D1024115

"Did you find out anything?" asked Happy Jack eagerly.
FRONTISPIECE. *See page 52.*

DOVER
CHILDREN'S THRIFT CLASSICS

The Adventures of Happy Jack

THORNTON W. BURGESS

Original Illustrations by Harrison Cady

PUBLISHED IN ASSOCIATION WITH THE
THORNTON W. BURGESS MUSEUM AND THE
GREEN BRIAR NATURE CENTER, SANDWICH, MASSACHUSETTS,
BY
DOVER PUBLICATIONS, INC., MINEOLA, NEW YORK

DOVER CHILDREN'S THRIFT CLASSICS
EDITOR OF THIS VOLUME: JANET BAINE KOPITO

Copyright

Copyright © 2004 by Dover Publications, Inc.
All rights reserved.

Bibliographical Note

This Dover edition, first published in 2004 in association with the Thornton W. Burgess Museum and the Green Briar Nature Center, Sandwich, Massachusetts, who have provided a new introduction, is an unabridged republication of the work originally published by Little, Brown, and Company, Boston, in 1918.

Library of Congress Cataloging-in-Publication Data

Burgess, Thornton W. (Thornton Waldo), 1874–1965.
The adventures of Happy Jack / Thornton W. Burgess ; original illustrations by Harrison Cady.
p. cm. — (Dover children's thrift classics)
"Published in association with the Thornton W. Burgess Museum and the Green Briar Nature Center, Sandwich, Massachusetts."
Summary: In his adventures in the Green Forest, Happy Jack Squirrel learns to share his hickory nuts with Chatterer the Red Squirrel and Striped Chipmunk and hide with Farmer Brown's boy to escape from Shadow the Weasel.
ISBN 0-486-43321-8 (pbk.)
[1. Gray squirrel—Fiction. 2. Squirrels—Fiction. 3. Forest animals—Fiction. 4. Forests and forestry—Fiction.] I. Cady, Harrison, 1877– ill. II. Title. III. Series.

PZ7.B917Abo 2004
[Fic]—dc22

2004041439

Manufactured in the United States of America
Dover Publications, Inc., 31 East 2nd Street, Mineola, N.Y. 11501

Introduction to the Dover Edition

In 1918, Thornton W. Burgess wrote *The Adventures of Happy Jack,* his thirty-eighth children's book. Mr. Burgess was an author and naturalist who wrote over 170 books for children. In this story, Happy Jack Squirrel and his cousin, Chatterer the Red Squirrel, are quarreling over hickory nuts. They are so busy deciding who has the rights to the nuts that they don't even notice Striped Chipmunk taking all of them! Learn why Happy Jack becomes fond of Farmer Brown's boy, and why Shadow the Weasel gets a new home.

Everyone knows that Happy Jack Squirrel is very thrifty. Each fall, Happy Jack starts to store food to eat during the long winter months. In fact, Mr. Burgess used Happy Jack as a symbol of patriotism during World War I. He believed that, in this way, he could help with the war effort. The Happy Jack Thrift Club was started as a way for children to learn what they could, and should, do to help their country during a time of great need. Buttons were given out with the purchase of twenty-five-cent thrift stamps, sixteen of which could be redeemed for a war-savings stamp, along with a certificate of membership and a booklet of Happy Jack stories.

Thousands of children across the country participated in this program. Even President Woodrow Wilson was a member of the Happy Jack Thrift Club.

Mr. Burgess dedicated this book to the renowned wildlife conservationist Dr. William Hornaday. Dr. Hornaday is credited with saving the American bison and other wildlife species from extinction. He also helped to found the National Zoo in Washington, D.C., as well as the New York Zoological Society. Thornton Burgess worked with Dr. Hornaday to protect migratory birds. Thornton Burgess was also the recipient of the Wild Life Protection Medal for distinguished service to wildlife, an award that was later named for Dr. Hornaday after his death.

You can learn more about the life of Thornton Burgess, his writings, and conservation efforts by visiting the Thornton Burgess Museum or the Green Briar Nature Center in Sandwich, Massachusetts, or online at www.thorntonburgess.org. The Thornton W. Burgess Society, a nonprofit educational organization founded in 1976 to "inspire reverence for wildlife and concern for the natural environment," operates the Museum, Green Briar, and the East Sandwich Game Farm.

Contents

List of Illustrations

TO

DR. WILLIAM T. HORNADAY

TO WHOM POSTERITY WILL OWE A DEBT OF GRATITUDE FOR HIS VALIANT FIGHT TO PRESERVE AMERICAN WILD LIFE, WHO HAS BEEN A LIFELONG CHAMPION OF HAPPY JACK SQUIRREL, AND TO WHOM THE AUTHOR IS DEEPLY INDEBTED FOR ENCOURAGEMENT AND ASSISTANCE THIS BOOK IS GRATEFULLY DEDICATED

The Adventures of Happy Jack

I
Happy Jack Drops a Nut

> Save a little every day,
> And for the future put away.
>
> *Happy Jack.*

Happy Jack Squirrel sat on the tip of one of the highest branches of a big hickory tree. Happy Jack was up very early that morning. In fact, jolly, round, red Mr. Sun was still in his bed behind the Purple Hills when Happy Jack hopped briskly out of bed. He washed himself thoroughly and was ready for business by the time Mr. Sun began his climb up in the blue, blue sky.

You see, Happy Jack had found that big hickory tree just loaded with nuts all ripe and ready to gather. He was quite sure that no one else had found that special tree, and he wanted to get all the nuts before any one else found out about them. So he was all ready and off he raced to the big tree just as soon as it was light enough to see.

> "The nuts that grow in the hickory tree—
> They're all for me! They're all for me!"

Happy Jack was humming that little song as he rested for a few minutes 'way up in the top of the tree and wondered if his storehouse would hold all these big, fat nuts. Just then he heard a great scolding a little way over in the Green Forest. Happy Jack stopped humming and listened. He knew that voice. It was his cousin's voice—the voice of Chatterer the Red Squirrel. Happy Jack frowned. "I hope he won't come over this way," muttered Happy Jack. He does not love his cousin Chatterer anyway, and then there was the big tree full of hickory nuts! He didn't want Chatterer to find that.

I am afraid that Happy Jack was selfish. There were more nuts than he could possibly eat in one winter, and yet he wasn't willing that his cousin, Chatterer the Red Squirrel, should have a single one. Now Chatterer is short-tempered and a great scold. Some one or something had upset him this morning, and he was scolding as fast as his tongue could go, as he came running right towards the tree in which Happy Jack was sitting. Happy Jack sat perfectly still and watched. He didn't move so much as the tip of his big gray tail. Would Chatterer go past and not see that big tree full of nuts? It looked very much as if he would, for he was so busy scolding that he wasn't paying much attention to other things.

Happy Jack smiled as Chatterer came running under the tree without once looking up. He was so tickled that he started to hug himself and didn't remember that he was holding a big, fat nut in his hands. Of course he dropped it. Where do you think it went? Well, Sir, it fell straight down, down from the top of that tall tree, and it landed right on the head of Chatterer the Red Squirrel!

"My stars!" cried Chatterer, stopping his scolding and his running together, and rubbing his head where the nut had hit him. Then he looked up to see where it had come from. Of course, he looked straight up at Happy Jack.

"You did that purposely!" screamed Chatterer, his short temper flaring up.

"I didn't!" snapped Happy Jack.

"You did!"

"I didn't!"

Oh, dear, oh, dear, such a sight! two little Squirrels, one in a gray suit and one in a red suit, contradicting each other and calling names! It was such a sad, sad sight, for you know they were cousins.

II
The Quarrel

It's up to you and up to me
To see how thrifty we can be.
To do our bit like soldiers true
It's up to me and up to you.

Happy Jack.

Two angry little people were making a dreadful noise in the Green Forest. It was a beautiful morning, a very beautiful fall morning, but all the beauty of it was being spoiled by the dreadful noise of these two little people. You see they were quarreling. Yes, Sir, they were quarreling, and it wasn't at all nice to see or nice to hear.

You know who they were. One was Happy Jack Squirrel, who wears a coat of gray, and the other was Chatterer the Red Squirrel, who always wears a red coat with vest of white. When Happy Jack had dropped that nut from the tip-top of the tall hickory tree and it had landed right on top of Chatterer's head it really had been an accident. All the time Happy Jack had been sitting as still as still could be, hoping that his cousin Chatterer would pass by without looking up and so seeing the big fat nuts in the top of that tree. You see Happy Jack was greedy and wanted all of them himself. Now Chatterer the Red Squirrel has a sharp temper, and also he has sharp eyes. All the time he was scolding Happy Jack and calling him names Chatterer's bright eyes were taking note of all those big, fat hickory nuts and his mouth began to water. Without wasting any more time he started up the tree to get some.

Happy Jack grew very angry, very angry indeed. He hurried down to meet Chatterer the Red Squirrel and to prevent him climbing the tree.

"You keep out of this tree; it's mine!" he shrieked.

"No such thing! You don't own the tree and I've got just as much right here as you have!" screamed Chatterer, dodging around to the other side of the tree.

"'Tis, too, mine! I found it first!" shouted Happy Jack. "You're a thief, so there!"

"I'm not!"

"You are!"

"You're a pig, Happy Jack! You're just a great big pig!"

"I'm not a pig! I found these nuts first and I tell you they're mine!" shrieked Happy Jack, so angry that every time he spoke he jerked his tail. And all the time he was chasing round and round the trunk of the tree trying to prevent Chatterer getting up.

Now Happy Jack is ever so much bigger than his cousin Chatterer but he isn't as spry. So in spite of him Chatterer got past, and like a little red flash was up in the top of the tree where the big, fat nuts were. But he didn't have time to pick even one, for after him came Happy Jack so angry that Chatterer knew that he would fare badly if Happy Jack should catch him. Round and round, over and across, this way and that way, in the top of the tall hickory tree raced Chatterer the Red Squirrel with his cousin, Happy Jack the Gray Squirrel, right at his heels, and calling him everything bad to be thought of. Yes, indeed it was truly dreadful, and Peter Rabbit, who happened along just then, put his hands over his ears so as not to hear such a dreadful quarrel.

Peter Rabbit, who happened along just then, put his hands over his ears. *See page 6.*

III
Striped Chipmunk Is Kept Very Busy

I prefer big acorns but I never refuse little ones.
They fit in between.

Happy Jack.

Striped Chipmunk was sitting just inside a hollow log, studying about how he could fill up his new storehouse for the winter. Striped Chipmunk is very thrifty. He likes to play, and he is one of the merriest of all the little people who live on the Green Meadows or in the Green Forest. He lives right on the edge of both and knows everybody, and everybody knows him. Almost every morning the Merry Little Breezes of Old Mother West Wind hurry over to have a frolic with him the very first thing. But though he dearly loves to play, he never lets play interfere with work. Whatever he does, be it play or work, he does with all his might.

"I love the sun; I love the rain;
I love to work; I love to play.
Whatever it may bring to me
I love each minute of each day."

So said Striped Chipmunk, as he sat in the hollow log and studied how he could fill that splendid big new storehouse. Pretty soon he pricked up his funny little ears. What was all that noise over in the Green Forest? Striped Chipmunk peeped out of the hollow log. Over in the top of a tall hickory tree a terrible fuss was going on. Striped Chipmunk listened. He heard angry voices, such angry voices! They were the voices of his big cousins, Happy Jack the Gray Squirrel and Chatterer the Red Squirrel.

"Dear me! Dear me! How those two do quarrel! I must go over and see what it is all about," thought Striped Chipmunk.

So, with a flirt of his funny, little tail, he scampered out of the hollow log and over to the tall hickory tree. He knew all about that tree. Many, many times he had looked up at the big fat nuts in the top of it, watching them grow bigger and fatter, and hoping that when they grew ripe, Old Mother West Wind would find time to shake them down to him. You know Striped Chipmunk is not much of a climber, and so he cannot go up and pick the nuts as do his big cousins, Happy Jack and Chatterer.

When he reached the tall hickory tree, what do you think was happening? Why, those big, fat nuts were rattling down to the ground on every side, just as if Old Mother West Wind was shaking the tree as hard as she could. But Old Mother West Wind wasn't there at all. No, Sir, there wasn't even one of the Merry Little Breezes up in the tree-tops. The big fat nuts were rattling down just on account of the dreadful quarrel of Striped Chipmunk's two foolish cousins, Happy Jack and Chatterer.

It was all because Happy Jack was greedy. Chatterer had climbed the tree, and now Happy Jack, who is bigger but not so spry, was chasing Chatterer round and round and over the tree-top, and both were so angry that they didn't once notice that they were knocking down the very nuts over which they were quarreling.

Striped Chipmunk didn't stop to listen to the quarrel. No, Sir-ee! He stuffed a big fat nut in each pocket in his cheeks and scampered back to his splendid new storehouse as fast as his little legs would take him. Back and forth, back and forth, scampered Striped Chipmunk, and all the time he was laughing inside and hoping his big cousins would keep right on quarreling.

IV
Happy Jack and Chatterer Feel Foolish

If you get and spend a penny,
Then of course you haven't any.
Be like me—a Happy Jack—
And put it where you'll get it back.

Happy Jack.

Happy Jack and Chatterer were out of breath. Happy Jack was puffing and blowing, for he is big and fat, and it is not so easy for him to race about in the tree-tops as it is for his smaller, slim, nimble cousin, Chatterer. So Happy Jack was the first to stop. He sat on a branch 'way up in the top of the tall hickory tree and glared across at Chatterer, who sat on a branch on the other side of the tall tree.

"Couldn't catch me, could you, smarty?" taunted Chatterer.

"You just wait until I do! I'll make you sorry you ever came near my hickory tree," snapped Happy Jack.

"I'm waiting. Besides, it isn't your tree any more than it's mine," replied Chatterer, and made a face at Happy Jack.

Happy Jack hopped up as if he meant to begin

the chase again, but he had a pain in his side from running so hard and so long, and so he sat down again. Right down in his heart Happy Jack knew that Chatterer was right, that the tree didn't belong to him any more than to his cousin. But when he thought of all those big, fat nuts with which the tall hickory tree had been loaded, greedy thoughts chased out all thoughts of right and he said to himself again, as he had said when he first saw his cousin, that Chatterer shouldn't have *one* of them. He stopped scolding long enough to steal a look at them, and then—what do you think Happy Jack did? Why, he gave such a jump of surprise that he nearly lost his balance. Not a nut was to be seen!

Happy Jack blinked. Then, he rubbed his eyes and looked again. He couldn't see a nut anywhere! There were the husks in which the nuts had grown big and fat until they were ripe, but now every husk was empty. Chatterer saw the queer look on Happy Jack's face, and he looked too. Now Chatterer the Red Squirrel had very quick wits, and he guessed right away what had happened. He knew that while they had been quarreling and racing over the top of the tall hickory tree, they must have knocked down all the nuts, which were just ready to fall anyway. Like a little red flash, Chatterer started down the tree. Then Happy Jack guessed too, and down he started as fast as he could go, crying, "Stop, thief!" all the way.

When he reached the ground, there was Chatterer scurrying around and poking under the fallen leaves, but he hadn't found a single nut. Happy Jack couldn't stop to quarrel any more, because you see he was afraid that Chatterer would find the biggest and fattest nuts, so he began to scurry around and hunt too. It was queer, very queer, how those nuts could have hidden so! They hunted and hunted, but no nuts were to be found. Then they stopped and stared up at the top of the tall hickory tree. Not a nut could they see. Then they stared at each other, and gradually a foolish, a very foolish look crept over each face.

"Where—where do you suppose they have gone?" asked Happy Jack in a queer-sounding voice.

Just then they heard some one laughing fit to kill himself. It was Peter Rabbit.

"Did you take our hickory nuts?" they both shouted angrily.

"No," replied Peter, "no, I didn't take them, though they were not yours, anyway!" And then he went off into another fit of laughter, for Peter had seen Striped Chipmunk very hard at work taking away those very nuts while his two big cousins had been quarreling in the tree-top.

V
Happy Jack Suspects Striped Chipmunk

Thrift is one test of true loyalty to your country.
Happy Jack.

Happy Jack didn't look happy a bit. Indeed, Happy Jack looked very unhappy. You see, he looked just as he felt. He had set his heart on having all the big, fat nuts that he had found in the top of that tall hickory tree, and now, instead of having all of them, he hadn't any of them. Worse still, he knew right down in his heart that it was his own fault. He had been too greedy. But what *had* become of those nuts?

Happy Jack was studying about this as he sat with his back against a big chestnut tree. He remembered how hard Peter Rabbit had laughed when Happy Jack and his cousin, Chatterer the Red Squirrel, had been so surprised because they could not find the nuts they had knocked down. Peter hadn't taken them, for Peter has no use for them, but he must know what had become of them, for he was still laughing as he had gone off down the Lone Little Path. While he was thinking of all this, Happy Jack's bright eyes had been wide open, as they usually are, so that no danger should come near. Suddenly they saw something moving among the brown-and-yellow leaves on the ground. Happy Jack looked sharply, and then a sudden thought popped into his head.

"Hi, there, Cousin Chipmunk," he shouted.

"Hi, there, your own self!" replied Striped Chipmunk, for it was he.

"What are you doing down there?" asked Happy Jack.

"Looking for hickory nuts," replied Striped Chipmunk, and his eyes twinkled as he said it, for there wasn't a hickory tree near.

Happy Jack looked hard at Striped Chipmunk, for that sudden thought which had popped into his head when he first saw Striped Chipmunk was growing into a strong, a very strong, suspicion that Striped Chipmunk knew something about those lost hickory nuts. But Striped Chipmunk looked back at him so innocently that Happy Jack didn't know just what to think.

"Have you begun to fill your storehouse for winter yet?" inquired Happy Jack.

"Of course I have. I don't mean to let Jack Frost catch me with an empty storehouse," replied Striped Chipmunk.

"When leaves turn yellow, brown, and red,
And nuts come pitter, patter down;
When days are short and swiftly sped,
And Autumn wears her colored gown,

I'm up before old Mr. Sun
His nightcap has a chance to doff,
And have my day's work well begun
When others kick their bedclothes off."

"What are you filling your storehouse with?" asked Happy Jack, trying not to show too much interest.

"Corn, nice ripe yellow corn, and seeds and acorns and chestnuts," answered Striped Chipmunk. "And now I'm looking for some big, fat hickory nuts," he added, and his bright eyes twinkled. "Have you seen any, Happy Jack?"

Happy Jack said that he hadn't seen any, and Striped Chipmunk remarked that he couldn't waste any more time talking, and scurried away. Happy Jack watched him go, a puzzled little frown puckering up his brows.

"I believe he knows something about those nuts. I think I'll follow him and have a peep into his storehouse," he muttered.

VI
Happy Jack Spies on Striped Chipmunk

It's more important to mind your own affairs than to know what your neighbors are doing, but not nearly so interesting.

Happy Jack.

Striped Chipmunk was whisking about among the brown-and-yellow leaves that covered the ground on the edge of the Green Forest. He is such a little fellow that he looked almost like a brown leaf himself, and when one of Old Mother West Wind's Merry Little Breezes whirled the brown leaves in a mad little dance around him, it was the hardest work in the world to see Striped Chipmunk at all. Anyway, Happy Jack Squirrel found it so.

You see, Happy Jack was spying on Striped Chipmunk. Yes, Sir, Happy Jack was spying. Spying, you know, is secretly watching other people and trying to find out what they are doing. It isn't a nice thing to do, not a bit nice. Happy Jack knew it, and all the time he was doing it, he was feeling very much ashamed of himself. But he said to himself that he just *had* to know where Striped Chipmunk's storehouse was, because he just *had* to peep inside and find out if it held any of the big, fat hickory nuts that had disappeared from under the tall hickory tree while he was quarreling up in the top of it with his cousin, Chatterer the Red Squirrel.

But spying on Striped Chipmunk isn't the easiest thing in the world. Happy Jack was finding it the hardest work he had ever undertaken. Striped Chipmunk is so spry, and whisks about so, that you need eyes all around your head to keep track of him. Happy Jack found that his two eyes, bright and quick as they are, couldn't keep that little elf of a cousin of his always in sight. Every few minutes he would disappear and then bob up again in the most unexpected place and most provoking way.

> "Now I'm here, and now I'm there!
> Now I am not anywhere!
> Watch me now, for here I go
> Out of sight! I told you so!"

With the last words, Striped Chipmunk was nowhere to be seen. It seemed as if the earth must have opened and swallowed him. But it hadn't, for two minutes later Happy Jack saw him flirting his funny little tail in the sauciest way as he scampered along an old log.

Happy Jack began to suspect that Striped Chipmunk was just having fun with him. What else could he mean by saying such things? And yet Happy Jack was sure that Striped Chipmunk hadn't seen him, for, all the time he was watching, Happy Jack had taken the greatest care to keep hidden himself. No, it couldn't be, it just couldn't be that Striped Chipmunk knew that he was anywhere about. He would just be patient a little longer, and he would surely see that smart little cousin of his go to his storehouse. So Happy Jack waited and watched.

VII
Striped Chipmunk Has Fun with Happy Jack

Thrift is the meat in the nut of success.
Happy Jack.

Striped Chipmunk would shout in his shrillest voice:

"Hipperty, hopperty, one, two, three!
What do you think becomes of me?"

Then he would vanish from sight all in the wink of an eye. You couldn't tell where he went to. At least Happy Jack couldn't, and his eyes are sharper than yours or mine. Happy Jack was spying, you remember. He was watching Striped Chipmunk without letting Striped Chipmunk know it. At least he thought he was. But really he wasn't. Those sharp twinkling eyes of Striped Chipmunk see everything. You know, he is such a very little fellow that he has to be very wide-awake to keep out of danger.

And he *is* wide-awake. Oh, my, yes, indeed! When he is awake, and that is every minute of the daytime, he is the most wide-awake little fellow you ever did see. He had seen Happy Jack the very first thing, and he had guessed right away that Happy

Jack was spying on him so as to find out if he had any of the big, fat hickory nuts. Now Striped Chipmunk had *all* of those fat hickory nuts safely hidden in his splendid new storehouse, but he didn't intend to let Happy Jack know it. So he just pretended not to see Happy Jack, or to know that he was anywhere near, but acted as if he was just going about his own business. Really he was just having the best time ever fooling Happy Jack.

"The corn is ripe; the nuts do fall;
Acorns are sweet and plump.
I soon will have my storehouse full
Inside the hollow stump."

Striped Chipmunk sang this just as if no one was anywhere near, and he was singing just for joy. Of course Happy Jack heard it and he grinned.

"So your storehouse is in a hollow stump, my smart little cousin!" said Happy Jack to himself. "If that's the case, I'll soon find it."

Striped Chipmunk scurried along, and now he took pains to always keep in sight. Happy Jack followed, hiding behind the trees. Pretty soon Striped Chipmunk picked up a plump acorn and put it in the pocket of his right cheek. Then he picked up another and put that in the pocket in his left cheek. Then he crowded another into each; and his face was swelled so that you would hardly have guessed that it was Striped Chipmunk if you had chanced to meet him. My, my, he was a funny sight!

Happy Jack grinned again as he watched, partly because Striped Chipmunk looked so funny, and partly because he knew that if Striped Chipmunk was going to eat the acorns right away, he wouldn't stuff them into the pockets in his cheeks. But he had done this very thing, and so he must be going to take them to his storehouse.

Off scampered Striped Chipmunk, and after him stole Happy Jack, his eyes shining with excitement. Pretty soon he saw an old stump which looked as if it must be hollow. Happy Jack grinned more than ever as he carefully hid himself and watched. Striped Chipmunk scrambled up on the old stump, looked this way and that way, as if to be sure that no one was watching him, then with a flirt of his funny little tail he darted into a little round doorway. He was gone a long time, but by and by out he popped, looked this way and that way, and then scampered off in the direction from which he had come. Happy Jack didn't try to follow him. He waited until he was sure that Striped Chipmunk was out of sight and hearing, and then he walked over to the old stump.

"It's his storehouse fast enough," said Happy Jack.

VIII
Happy Jack Turns Burglar

As trees from little acorns, so
Great sums from little pennies grow.

Happy Jack.

Happy Jack Squirrel stood in front of the old stump into which he had seen Striped Chipmunk go with the pockets in his cheeks full of acorns, and out of which he had come with the pockets of his cheeks quite empty.

"It certainly is his storehouse, and now I'll find out if he is the one who got all those big, fat hickory nuts," muttered Happy Jack.

First he looked this way, and then he looked that way, to be sure that no one saw him, for what he was planning to do was a very dreadful thing, and he knew it. Happy Jack was going to turn burglar. A burglar, you know, is one who breaks into another's house or barn to steal, which is a very, very dreadful thing to do. Yet this is just what Happy Jack Squirrel was planning to do. He was going to get into that old stump, and if those big, fat hickory nuts were there, as he was sure they were, he was going to take them. He tried very hard to make himself believe that it wouldn't be stealing. He had watched those nuts in the top of the tall hickory tree so long that he had grown to think that they belonged to him. Of course they didn't, but he had made himself think they did.

Happy Jack walked all around the old stump, and then he climbed up on top of it. There was only one doorway, and that was the little round hole through which Striped Chipmunk had entered and then come out. It was too small for Happy Jack to even get his head through, though his cousin, Chatterer the Red Squirrel, who is much smaller, could have slipped in easily. Happy Jack sniffed and sniffed. He could smell nuts and corn and other good things. My, how good they did smell! His eyes shone greedily.

Happy Jack took one more hasty look around to see that no one was watching, then with his long sharp teeth he began to make the doorway larger. The wood was tough, but Happy Jack worked with might and main, for he wanted to get those nuts and get away before Striped Chipmunk should return, or any one else should happen along and see him. Soon the hole was big enough for him to get his head inside. It was a storehouse, sure enough. Happy Jack worked harder than ever, and soon the hole was large enough for him to get wholly inside.

What a sight! There was corn! and there were chestnuts and acorns! and there were a few hickory nuts, though these did not look so big and fat as the ones Happy Jack was looking for! Happy Jack chuckled to himself, a wicked, greedy chuckle, as he looked. And then something happened.

"Oh! Oh! Stop it! Leave me alone!" yelled Happy Jack.

IX
Happy Jack Squirrel's Sad Mistake

A Squirrel always is thrifty. Be as wise as a Squirrel.
Happy Jack.

"Let me go! Let me go!" yelled Happy Jack, as he backed out of the hollow stump faster than he had gone in, a great deal faster. Can you guess why? I'll tell you. It was because he was being pulled out. Yes, Sir, Happy Jack Squirrel was being pulled out by his big, bushy tail.

Happy Jack was more frightened than hurt. To be sure, it is not at all comfortable to have one's tail pulled, but Happy Jack wouldn't have minded this so much had it not been so unexpected, or if he could have seen who was pulling it. And then, right inside Happy Jack didn't feel a bit good. Why? Well, because he was doing a dreadful thing, and he *knew* that it was a dreadful thing. He had broken into somebody's storehouse to steal. He was sure that it was Striped Chipmunk's storehouse, and he wouldn't admit to himself that he was going to steal, actually *steal.* But all the time, right down deep in his heart, he knew that if he took any of those hickory nuts it would be stealing.

But Happy Jack had been careless. When he had

made the doorway big enough for him to crawl inside, he had left his tail hanging outside. Some one had very, very softly stolen up and grabbed it and begun to pull. It was so sudden and unexpected that Happy Jack yelled with fright. When he could get his wits together, he thought of course Striped Chipmunk had come back and was pulling his tail. When he thought that, he got over his fright right away, for Striped Chipmunk is such a little fellow that Happy Jack knew that he had nothing to fear from him.

So as fast as he could, Happy Jack backed out of the hole and whirled around. Of course he expected to face a very angry little Chipmunk. But he didn't. No, Sir, he didn't. Instead, he looked right into the angry face of his other cousin, Chatterer the Red Squirrel. And Chatterer *was* angry! Oh my, my, how angry Chatterer was! For a minute he couldn't find his voice, because his anger fairly choked him. And when he did, how his tongue did fly!

"You thief! You robber! What are you doing in my storehouse?" he shrieked.

Happy Jack backed away hurriedly, for though he is much bigger than Chatterer, he has a very wholesome respect for Chatterer's sharp teeth, and when he is very angry, Chatterer is a great fighter.

"I—I didn't know it was your storehouse," said Happy Jack, backing away still further.

"It doesn't make any difference if you didn't; you're a thief just the same!" screamed Chatterer and rushed at Happy Jack. And what do you think Happy Jack did? Why, he just turned tail and ran, Chatterer after him, crying "Thief! Robber! Coward!" at the top of his lungs, so that every one in the Green Forest could hear.

X
Striped Chipmunk's Happy Thought

Waste seems to me a dreadful sin;
It works to lose and not to win.

Thrift will win; it cannot lose.
Between them 'tis for you to choose.
Happy Jack.

Striped Chipmunk sat on a mossy old log, laughing until his sides ached. "Ha, ha, ha! Ho, ho, ho! Oh, dear! Oh, dear! Ho, ho, ho, ho, ho!" laughed Striped Chipmunk, holding his sides. Over in the Green Forest he could still hear Chatterer the Red Squirrel crying "Thief! Robber!" as he chased his big cousin, Happy Jack, and every time he heard it, Striped Chipmunk laughed harder.

You see, Striped Chipmunk had known all the time that Happy Jack was spying on him, and he had had no end of fun fooling Happy Jack by suddenly disappearing and then bobbing into view. He had known that Happy Jack was following him so as to find out where his storehouse was. Then Striped Chipmunk had remembered the storehouse of Chatterer the Red Squirrel. He had filled the pockets in his cheeks with acorns and gone straight over to Chatterer's storehouse and put them inside, knowing that Happy Jack would follow him and would think that that was his storehouse. And that is just what happened.

Then Striped Chipmunk had hidden himself where he could see all that happened. He had seen Happy Jack look all around, to make sure that no one was near, and then tear open the little round doorway of Chatterer's storehouse until it was big enough for him to squeeze through. He had seen Chatterer come up, fly into a rage, and pull Happy Jack out by the tail. Indeed, he had had to clap both hands over his mouth to keep from laughing out loud. Then Happy Jack had turned tail and run away with Chatterer after him, shouting "Thief" and "Robber" at the top of his voice, and this had tickled Striped Chipmunk still more, for he knew that Chatterer himself is one of the greatest thieves in the Green Forest. So he sat on the mossy old log and laughed and laughed and laughed.

Finally Striped Chipmunk wiped the tears from his eyes and jumped up. "My, my, this will never do!" said he.

> "Idle hands and idle feet
> Never filled a storehouse yet;
> But instead, so I've heard say,
> Into mischief surely get."

"Here it is almost Thanksgiving and ——" Striped Chipmunk stopped and scratched his head, while a funny little pleased look crept into his face. "I wonder if Happy Jack and Chatterer would come to a Thanksgiving dinner," he muttered. "I believe I'll ask them just for fun."

Then Striped Chipmunk hurried home full of his new idea and chuckled as he planned his Thanksgiving dinner. Of course he couldn't have it at his own house. That wouldn't do at all. In the first place, the doorway would be altogether too small for Happy Jack. Anyway, his home was a secret, his very own secret, and he didn't propose to let Happy Jack and Chatterer know where it was, even for a Thanksgiving dinner. Then he thought of the big, smooth, mossy log he had been sitting on that very morning.

"The very place!" cried Striped Chipmunk, and scurried away to find Happy Jack Squirrel and Chatterer the Red Squirrel to invite them to his Thanksgiving dinner.

XI
Striped Chipmunk's Thanksgiving Dinner

There's nothing quite so sweet in life
As making up and ending strife.

Happy Jack.

Striped Chipmunk jumped out of bed very early Thanksgiving morning. It was going to be a very busy day. He had invited Happy Jack the Gray Squirrel, and Chatterer the Red Squirrel, to eat Thanksgiving dinner with him, and each had promised to be there. Striped Chipmunk chuckled as he thought how neither of his guests knew that the other was to be there. He washed his face and hands, brushed his hair, and ate his breakfast. Then he scurried over to his splendid new storehouse, which no one knew of but himself, and stuffed the pockets in his cheeks with good things to eat. When he couldn't stuff another thing in, he scurried over to the nice, mossy log on the edge of the Green Forest, and there he emptied his pockets, for that was to be his dining table.

Back and forth, back and forth between his secret storehouse and the smooth, mossy log hurried Striped Chipmunk. He knew that Happy Jack and the Chatterer have great appetites, and he wanted to be sure that there was plenty of good things to eat. And as he scurried along, he sang a little song.

"Thanksgiving comes but once a year,
But when it comes it brings good cheer.
For in my storehouse on this day
Are piles of good things hid away.
Each day I've worked from early morn
To gather acorns, nuts, and corn,
Till now I've plenty and to spare
Without a worry or a care.
So light of heart the whole day long,
I'll sing a glad Thanksgiving song."

Promptly at the dinner hour Happy Jack appeared coming from one direction, and Chatterer the Red Squirrel coming from another direction. They didn't see each other until just as they reached Striped Chipmunk's smooth, mossy log. Then they stopped and scowled. Striped Chipmunk pretended not to notice anything wrong and bustled about, talking all the time as if his guests were the best of friends.

On the smooth, mossy log was a great pile of shining yellow corn. There was another pile of plump ripe acorns, and three little piles of dainty looking brown seeds. But the thing that Happy Jack couldn't keep his eyes off was right in the middle. It was a huge pile of big, fat hickory nuts. Now who could remain ill-tempered and cross with such a lot of goodies spread before him? Certainly not Happy Jack or his cousin, Chatterer the Red Squirrel. They just had to smile in spite of themselves, and when Striped Chipmunk urged them to sit down and help themselves, they did. In three minutes they were so busy eating that they had forgotten all about their quarrel and were laughing and chatting like the best of friends.

"It's quite a family party, isn't it?" said Striped Chipmunk, for you know they are all cousins.

Whitefoot the Wood Mouse happened along, and Striped Chipmunk insisted that he should join the party. Later Sammy Jay came along, and nothing would excuse him from sharing in the feast, too. When everybody had eaten and eaten until they couldn't hold another thing, and it was time to think of going home, Striped Chipmunk insisted that Happy Jack and Chatterer should divide between them the big, fat hickory nuts that were left, and they did without once quarreling about it.

> "Thanksgiving comes but once a year,
> And when it comes it brings good cheer,"

said Striped Chipmunk to himself as he watched his guests depart.

XII
Happy Jack Does Some Thinking

To call another a thief doesn't make him one.

Happy Jack.

Happy Jack sat up in a chestnut tree, and his face was very sober. The fact is, Happy Jack was doing some very hard thinking. This is so very unusual for him that Sammy Jay stopped to ask if he was sick. You see he is naturally a happy-go-lucky little scamp, and that is one reason that he is called Happy Jack. But this morning he was thinking and thinking hard, so hard, in fact, that he almost lost his temper when Sammy Jay interrupted his thoughts with such a foolish question.

What was he thinking about? Can you not guess? Why, he was thinking about those big, fat hickory nuts that Striped Chipmunk had had for his Thanksgiving dinner, and how Striped Chipmunk had given him some of them to bring home. He was very sure that they were the very same nuts that he had watched grow big and fat in the top of the tall hickory tree and then had knocked down while chasing his cousin, Chatterer. When they had reached the ground and found the nuts gone, Happy Jack had at once suspected that Striped

Chipmunk had taken them, and now he felt sure about it.

But all at once things looked very different to Happy Jack, and the more he thought about how he had acted, the more ashamed of himself he grew.

"There certainly must have been enough of those nuts for all of us, and if I hadn't been so greedy we might all have had a share. As it is, I've got only those that Striped Chipmunk gave me, and Chatterer has only those that Striped Chipmunk gave him. It must be that that sharp little cousin of mine with the striped coat has got the rest, and I guess he deserves them."

Then all of a sudden Happy Jack realized how Striped Chipmunk had fooled him into thinking that the storehouse of Chatterer was his storehouse, and Happy Jack began to laugh. The more he thought of it, the harder he laughed.

"The joke certainly is on me!" he exclaimed. "The joke certainly is on me, and it served me right. Hereafter I'll mind my own business. If I had spent half as much time looking for hickory nuts as I did looking for Striped Chipmunk's storehouse, I would be ready for winter now, and Chatterer couldn't call me a thief."

Then he laughed again as he thought how Striped Chipmunk must have enjoyed seeing him pulled out of Chatterer's storehouse by the tail.

"What's the joke?" asked Bobby Coon, who happened along just then.

"I've just learned a lesson," replied Happy Jack.

"What is it?" asked Bobby.

Happy Jack grinned as he answered:

"I've found that greed will never, never pay.
It makes one cross and ugly, and it drives one's
friends away.
And being always selfish and always wanting more,
One's very apt to lose the things that one has had
before."

"Pooh!" said Bobby Coon. "Have you just found that out? I learned that a long time ago."

XIII
Happy Jack Gets a Warning

It matters not how smart you are,
So be it you are heedless too.
It isn't what you know that counts
So much as what it is to you.

Happy Jack.

A fat Gray Squirrel is very tempting to a number of people in the Green Forest, particularly in winter, when getting a living is hard work. Almost every day Reddy and Granny Fox stole softly through that part of the Green Forest where Happy Jack Squirrel lived, hoping to surprise and catch him on the ground. But they never did. Roughleg the Hawk and Hooty the Owl wasted a great deal of time, sitting around near Happy Jack's home, hoping to catch him when he was not watching, but they never did.

Happy Jack knew all about these big hungry neighbors, and he was always on the watch for them. He knew their ways and just where they would be likely to hide. He took the greatest care to look into every such hiding place near at hand before he ventured down out of the trees, and because these hungry neighbors are so big, he never had any trouble in seeing them if they happened to be around. So Happy Jack didn't do much worrying about them. The fact is, Happy Jack wasn't afraid of them at all, for the simple reason that he knew they couldn't follow him into his hollow tree.

Having nuts stored away, he would have been perfectly happy but for one thing. Yes, Sir, there was only one thing to spoil Happy Jack's complete happiness, and that was the fear that Shadow the Weasel might take it into his head to pay him a visit. Shadow can go through a smaller hole then Happy Jack can, and so Happy Jack knew that while he was wholly safe from his other enemies, he wasn't safe at all from Shadow the Weasel. And this worried him. Yes, Sir, it worried Happy Jack. He hadn't seen or heard of Shadow for a long time, but he had a feeling that he was likely to turn up almost any time, especially now that everything was covered with snow and ice, and food was scarce and hard to get. He sometimes actually wished that he wasn't as fat as he was. Then he would be less tempting to his hungry neighbors.

But no good comes of worrying. No, Sir, not a bit of good comes of worrying, and Happy Jack knows it.

"All I can do is to watch out and not be careless," said he, and dropped the shell of a nut on the head of Reddy Fox, who happened to be passing under the tree in which Happy Jack was sitting. Reddy looked up and showed his teeth angrily. Happy Jack laughed and scampered away through the tree-tops to another part of the Green Forest where he had some very secret stores of nuts.

He was gone most of the day, and when he started back home he was in the best of spirits, for his stores had not been found by any one else. He was in such good spirits that for once he quite forgot Shadow the Weasel. He was just going to pop into his doorway without first looking inside, a very foolish thing to do, when he heard some one calling him. He turned to see Tommy Tit the Chickadee hurrying towards him, and it was very clear that Tommy was greatly excited.

"Hello, Tommy Tit! What ails you?" exclaimed Happy Jack.

"Don't go in there, Happy Jack!" cried Tommy Tit. "Shadow the Weasel is in there waiting for you!"

Happy Jack turned quite pale. "Are you sure?" he gasped.

Tommy Tit nodded as if he would nod his head off. "I saw him go in, and he hasn't come out, for I've kept watch," said he. "You better get away from here before he knows you are about."

That was good advice, but it was too late. Even as Tommy Tit spoke, a sharp face with red, angry eyes was thrust out of Happy Jack's doorway. It was the face of Shadow the Weasel.

XIV
Happy Jack's Run for Life

A coward he who runs away
When he should stay and fight,
But wise is he who knows when he
Should run with all his might.

Happy Jack.

It isn't cowardly to run away when it is quite useless to stay and fight. So it wasn't so cowardly of Happy Jack Squirrel to turn tail and run the instant he caught sight of Shadow the Weasel. No, Sir, it wasn't cowardly at all, although it might have looked so to you had you been there to see, for Happy Jack is bigger than Shadow. But when it comes to a fight, Happy Jack is no match at all for Shadow the Weasel, and he knows it. Shadow is too quick for him, and though Happy Jack were ever so brave, he would have no chance at all in a fight with Shadow.

And so the very instant he saw the cruel face of Shadow with its fierce red eyes glaring at him from his own doorway, Happy Jack turned tail and ran. Yes, Sir, that is just what he did, and it was the wisest thing he could have done. He hoped with a mighty hope that Shadow would not follow him, but he hoped in vain. Shadow had made up his mind to dine on Squirrel, and he didn't propose to see his dinner run away without trying to catch it. So the instant Happy Jack started, Shadow started after him, stopping only long enough to snarl an ugly threat at Tommy Tit the Chickadee, because Tommy had warned Happy Jack that Shadow was waiting for him.

But Tommy didn't mind that threat. Oh, my, no! Tommy didn't mind it at all. He can fly, and so he had no fear of Shadow the Weasel. But he was terribly afraid for Happy Jack. He knew, just as Happy Jack knew, that there wasn't a single place where Happy Jack could hide into which Shadow could not follow him. So Tommy flitted from tree to tree behind Happy Jack, hoping that in some way he might be able to help him.

From tree to tree raced Happy Jack, making desperately long leaps. Shadow the Weasel followed, and though he ran swiftly, he didn't appear to be hurrying, and he took no chances on those long leaps. If the leap was too long to take safely, Shadow simply ran back down the tree, across to the next one and up that. It didn't worry him at all that Happy Jack was so far ahead that he was out of sight. He knew that he could trust his nose to follow the scent of Happy Jack. In fact, it rather pleased him to have Happy Jack race away in such fright, for in that way he would soon tire himself out.

And this is just what Happy Jack did do. He ran and jumped and jumped and ran as fast as he could until he was so out of breath that he just had to stop for a rest. But he couldn't rest much. He was too terribly frightened. He shivered and shook while he got his breath, and never for a second did he take his eyes from his back trail. Presently he saw a slim white form darting along the snow straight towards the tree in which he was resting. Once more Happy Jack ran, and somehow he felt terribly helpless and hopeless.

He had to rest oftener now, and each rest was shorter than the one before, because, you know, Shadow was a less and less distance behind. Poor Happy Jack! He had tried every trick he knew, and not one of them had fooled Shadow the Weasel. Now he was too tired to run much farther. The last little bit of hope left Happy Jack's heart. He blinked his eyes very fast to keep back the tears, as he thought that this was probably the last time he would ever look at the beautiful Green Forest he loved so. Then he gritted his teeth and made up his mind that anyway he would fight his best, even if it was hopeless. It was just at that very minute that he heard the voice of Tommy Tit the Chickadee calling to him in great excitement, and somehow, he didn't know why, a wee bit of hope sprang up in his heart.

XV
Who Saved Happy Jack Squirrel?

Blessed he whose words of cheer
Help put hope in place of fear.

Happy Jack.

It never has been fully decided among the little people of the Green Forest and the Green Meadows just who really did save Happy Jack Squirrel. Some say that Tommy Tit the Chickadee deserves all the credit, and some say that—but wait. Let me tell you just what happened, and then perhaps you can decide for yourself who saved Happy Jack.

You see, it was this way: Happy Jack had run and run and run and tried every trick he knew to get away from Shadow the Weasel, but all in vain. At last he was so out of breath and so tired that he felt that he couldn't run any more. He had just made up his mind that he would wait right where he was for Shadow and then put up the best fight he could, even if it was hopeless, when he heard Tommy Tit calling to him in great excitement.

"Dee, dee, chickadee! Come here quick, Happy Jack! Come here quick!" called Tommy Tit.

A wee bit of hope sprang up in Happy Jack's heart. He couldn't imagine what possible help

Happy Jack tried every trick he knew to get away from Shadow the Weasel. *See page 44.*

Tommy Tit could be, but he would go see. So taking a long breath he started on as fast as he could in the direction of Tommy's voice. He couldn't run very fast, because, you know, he was so tired, but he did the best he could. Presently he saw Tommy just ahead of him flying about in great excitement.

"Dee, dee, dee, there he is! Go to him! Go to him, Happy Jack! Hurry! Hurry! Dee, dee, dee, oh, do hurry!" cried Tommy Tit.

For just a second Happy Jack didn't know what he meant. Then he saw Farmer Brown's boy watching Tommy Tit as if he didn't know what to make of the little fellow's excitement.

"Go to him! Go to him!" called Tommy. "He won't hurt you, and he won't let Shadow the Weasel hurt you! See me! See me! Dee, dee, see me!" And with that Tommy Tit flew right down on Farmer Brown's boy's hand, for you know he and Farmer Brown's boy are great friends.

Happy Jack hesitated. He knew that Farmer Brown's boy had tried to make friends with him, and every day since the ice and snow had come had put out nuts and corn for him, but he couldn't quite forget the old fear of him. He couldn't quite trust him. So now he hesitated. Then he looked back. Shadow the Weasel was only a few jumps behind him, and his little eyes glowed red and savage. Farmer Brown's boy might not hurt him, but Shadow certainly would. Shadow would kill him. Happy Jack made up his mind, and with a little gasp raced madly across the snow straight to Farmer Brown's boy and ran right up to his shoulder.

Shadow the Weasel had been so intent on catching Happy Jack that he hadn't noticed Farmer Brown's boy at all. Now he saw him for the first time and stopped short, snarling and spitting. Whatever else you may say of Shadow the Weasel, he is no coward. For a minute it looked as if he really meant to follow Happy Jack and get him in spite of Farmer Brown's boy, and Happy Jack trembled as he looked down into those angry little red eyes. But Shadow knows when he is well off, and now he knew better than to come a step nearer. So he snarled and spit, and then, as Farmer Brown's boy took a step forward, leaped to one side and disappeared in the old stone wall.

Very gently and softly Farmer Brown's boy talked to Happy Jack as he took him to the nearest tree. Then, when Happy Jack was safely up in the tree, he went over to the stone wall and tried to drive Shadow the Weasel out. He pulled over the stones until at last Shadow jumped out, and then Farmer Brown's boy chased him clear into the Green Forest.

"Dee, dee, dee, what did I tell you?" cried Tommy Tit happily, as he flew over to where Happy Jack was sitting.

Now who really saved Happy Jack—Tommy Tit or Farmer Brown's boy?

XVI
Happy Jack Misses Farmer Brown's Boy

One and one are always two,
And two and two are four.
And just as true it is you'll find
That love and love make more.

Happy Jack.

Go ask Happy Jack Squirrel. He knows. He knows because he has proved it. It began when Farmer Brown's boy saved him from Shadow the Weasel. Perhaps I should say when Farmer Brown's boy and Tommy Tit saved him, for if it hadn't been for Tommy, it never would have entered Happy Jack's head to run to Farmer Brown's boy. After that, of course, Happy Jack and Farmer Brown's boy became great friends. Farmer Brown's boy came over to the Green Forest every day to see Happy Jack, and always he had the most delicious nuts in his pockets. At first Happy Jack had been a wee bit shy. He couldn't quite get over that old fear he had had so long. Then he would remember how Farmer Brown's boy had saved him, and that would make him ashamed, and he would walk right up and take the nuts.

Farmer Brown's boy would talk to him in the

nicest way and tell him that he loved him, and that there wasn't the least thing in the world to be afraid of. Pretty soon Happy Jack began to love Farmer Brown's boy a little. He couldn't help it. He just had to love any one who was so kind and gentle to him. Now as soon as he began to love a little, and felt sure in his own heart that Farmer Brown's boy loved him a little, he found that love and love make more love, and it wasn't any time at all before he had become very fond of Farmer Brown's boy, so fond of him that he was almost jealous of Tommy Tit, who had been a friend of Farmer Brown's boy for a long time. It got so that Happy Jack looked forward each day to the visit of Farmer Brown's boy, and as soon as he heard his whistle, he would hasten to meet him. Some folks were unkind enough to say that it was just because of the nuts and corn he was sure to find in Farmer Brown's boy's pockets, but that wasn't so at all.

At last there came a day when he missed that cheery whistle. He waited and waited. At last he went clear to the edge of the Green Forest, but there was no whistle and no sign of Farmer Brown's boy. It was the same way the next day and the next. Happy Jack forgot to frisk about the way he usually does. He lost his appetite. He just sat around and moped.

When Tommy Tit the Chickadee came to call, as he did every day, Happy Jack found that Tommy was anxious too. Tommy had been up to Farmer

Brown's dooryard several times, and he hadn't seen anything of Farmer Brown's boy.

"I think he must have gone away," said Tommy.

"He would have come down here first and said good-by," replied Happy Jack.

"You—you don't suppose something has happened to him, do you?" asked Tommy.

"I don't know. I don't know what to think," replied Happy Jack, soberly. "Do you know, Tommy, I've grown very fond of Farmer Brown's boy."

"Of course. Dee, dee, dee, of course. Everybody who really knows him is fond of him. I've said all along that he is the best friend we've got, but no one seemed to believe me. I'm glad you've found it out for yourself. I tell you what, I'll go up to his house and have another look around." And without waiting for a reply, Tommy was off as fast as his little wings could take him.

"I hope, I do hope, that nothing has happened to him," mumbled Happy Jack, as he pretended to hunt for buried nuts while he waited for Tommy Tit to come back, and by "him" he meant Farmer Brown's boy.

XVII
Tommy Tit Brings News

No one knows too much, but many know too little.
Happy Jack.

Happy Jack very plainly was not happy. His name was the only happy thing about him. He fussed about on the edge of the Green Forest. He just couldn't keep still. When he thought anybody was looking, he pretended to hunt for some of the nuts he had buried in the fall, and dug holes down through the snow. But as soon as he thought that no one was watching, he would scamper up a tree where he could look over to Farmer Brown's house and look and look. It was very clear that Happy Jack was watching for some one and that he was anxious, very anxious, indeed.

It was getting late in the afternoon, and soon the Black Shadows would begin to creep out from the Purple Hills, behind which jolly, round, red Mr. Sun would go to bed. It would be bedtime for Happy Jack then, for you know he goes to bed very early, just as soon as it begins to get dark. The later it got, the more anxious and uneasy Happy Jack grew. He had just made up his mind that in a few minutes he would have to give up and go to bed when there was a flit of tiny wings, and Tommy Tit the Chickadee dropped into the tree beside him.

"Did you find out anything?" asked Happy Jack eagerly, before Tommy had a chance to say a word.

Tommy nodded. "He's there!" he panted, for he was quite out of breath from hurrying so.

"Where?" Happy Jack fairly shouted the question.

"Over there in the house," replied Tommy Tit.

"Then he hasn't gone away! It's just as I said, he hasn't gone away!" cried Happy Jack, and he was so relieved that he jumped up and down and as a result nearly tumbled out of the tree.

"No," replied Tommy, "he hasn't gone away, but I think there is something the matter with him."

Happy Jack grew very sober. "What makes you think so?" he demanded.

"If you'll give me time to get my breath, I'll tell you all about it," retorted Tommy Tit.

"All right, only please hurry," replied Happy Jack, and tried to look patient even if he wasn't.

Tommy Tit smoothed out some rumpled feathers and was most provokingly slow about it. "When I left here," he began at last, "I flew straight up to Farmer Brown's house, as I said I would. I flew all around it, but all I saw was that horrid Black Pussy on the back doorsteps, and she looked at me so hungrily that she made me dreadfully uncomfortable. I don't see what Farmer Brown keeps her about for, anyway."

"Never mind her; go on!" interrupted Happy Jack.

"Then I flew all around the barn, but I didn't see any one there but that ugly little upstart, Bully the English Sparrow, and he wanted to pick a fight with me right away." Tommy looked very indignant.

"Never mind him, go on!" cried Happy Jack impatiently.

"After that I flew back to the big maple tree close by the house," continued Tommy. "You know Farmer Brown's boy has kept a piece of suet tied in that tree all winter for me. I was hungry, and I thought I would get a bite to eat, but there wasn't any suet there. That pig of a Sammy Jay had managed to get it untied and had carried it all away. Of course that made me angry, and twice as hungry as before. I was trying to make up my mind what to do next when I happened to look over on the window sill, and what do you think I saw there?"

"What?" demanded Happy Jack eagerly.

"A lot of cracked hickory nuts!" declared Tommy. "I just knew that they were meant for me, and when I was sure that the way was clear, I flew over there. They tasted so good that I almost forgot about Farmer Brown's boy, when I just happened to look in the window. You know those windows are made of some queer stuff that looks like ice and isn't, and that you can see right through."

Happy Jack didn't know, for he never had been near enough to see, but he nodded, and Tommy Tit went on.

"There were many queer things inside, and I was wondering what they could be when all of a sudden I saw *him*. He was lying down, and there was something the matter with him. I tapped on the window to him and then I hurried back here."

XVIII
Happy Jack Decides to Make a Call

You'll find when all is said and done
Two heads are better far than one.

Happy Jack.

Happy Jack Squirrel hadn't slept very well. He had had bad dreams. Ever so many times in the night he had waked up, a very unusual thing for Happy Jack. The fact is, he had something on his mind. Yes, Sir, Happy Jack had something on his mind, and that something was Farmer Brown's boy. He often had had Farmer Brown's boy on his mind before, but in a very different way. Then it had been in the days when Farmer Brown's boy hunted through the Green Forest and over the Green Meadows with his terrible gun. Then everybody had Farmer Brown's boy on their minds most of the time. Happy Jack had hated him then, hated him because he had feared him. You know fear almost always leads to hate.

But now it was different. Farmer Brown's boy had put away his terrible gun. Happy Jack no longer feared him. Love had taken the place of hate in his heart, for had not Farmer Brown's boy saved him from Shadow the Weasel, and brought him nuts and corn when food was scarce? And now Tommy Tit had brought word that something was the matter with Farmer Brown's boy. It was this that was on Happy Jack's mind and had given him such a bad night.

As soon as it was daylight, Happy Jack scrambled out of bed to look for Tommy Tit. He didn't have long to wait, for Tommy is quite as early a riser as Happy Jack.

"Dee, dee, chickadee!
I hope you feel as well as me!"

sang Tommy merrily, as he flitted over to where Happy Jack was looking for his breakfast. The very sound of Tommy's voice made Happy Jack feel better. One must feel very badly indeed not to be a little more cheerful when Tommy Tit is about. The fact is, Tommy Tit packs about so much good cheer in that small person of his, that no one can be downhearted when he is about.

"Hello, Tommy," said Happy Jack. "If I could make other people feel as good as you do, do you know what I would do?"

"What?" asked Tommy.

"I'd go straight up to Farmer Brown's house and try to cheer up Farmer Brown's boy," replied Happy Jack.

"That's the very thing I have in mind," chuckled Tommy. "I've come over here to see if you won't come along with me. I've been up to his house so often that he won't think half so much of a visit from me as he will from you. Will you do it?"

Happy Jack looked a little startled. You see, he never had been over to Farmer Brown's house, and somehow he couldn't get over the idea that it would be a very dangerous thing to do. "I—I—do you really suppose I could?" he asked.

"I'm sure of it," replied Tommy Tit. "There's no one to be afraid of but Black Pussy and Bowser the Hound, and it's easy enough to keep out of their way. You can hide in the old stone wall until the way is clear and then run across to the big maple tree close to the house. Then you can look right in and see Farmer Brown's boy, and he can look out and see you. Will you do it?"

Happy Jack thought very hard for a few minutes. Then he made up his mind. "I'll do it!" said he in a very decided tone of voice. "Let's start right away."

"Good for you! Dee, dee, good for you!" cried Tommy Tit, and started to lead the way.

XIX
Tommy Tit and Happy Jack Pay a Visit

As grows the mighty elm tree,
From just a tiny seed,
So often great things happen
From just a kindly deed.

Happy Jack.

Great things were happening to Happy Jack Squirrel. He was actually on his way to Farmer Brown's house, and he had a feeling that other things were likely to happen when he got there. Now you may not think that it was anything very great that Happy Jack should be on his way to Farmer Brown's house. Very likely you are saying, "Pooh! that's nothing!" This may be true, and then again it may not. Suppose you do a little supposing. Suppose you had all your life been terribly afraid of a great giant fifty times bigger than you. Suppose that great giant had stopped hunting you and by little deeds of kindness had at last won your love. Suppose you learned that something was the matter with him, and you made up your mind to visit him at his great castle where there were other great giants whom you did not know. Wouldn't you think that great things were happening to you?

Well, that is exactly the way it was with Happy Jack Squirrel, as he and Tommy Tit the Chickadee started to go over to Farmer Brown's house to look for Farmer Brown's boy. Tommy Tit had been there often, so he didn't think anything about it, but Happy Jack never had been there, and if the truth were known, his heart was going pitapat, pitapat, with excitement and perhaps just a little fear. Through the Old Orchard they went, Tommy Tit flitting ahead and keeping a sharp watch for danger. When they reached the old stone wall on the edge of Farmer Brown's dooryard, Tommy told Happy Jack to hide there while he went to see if the way was clear. He was back in a few minutes.

"Dee, dee, everything is all right," said he. "Bowser the Hound is eating his breakfast out back where he can't see you at all, and Black Pussy is nowhere about. All you have to do is to follow me over to that big tree close to the house, and I will show you where Farmer Brown's boy is."

"I—I'm afraid," confessed Happy Jack.

"Pooh! There's nothing to be afraid of," asserted Tommy Tit in the most positive way. "Don't be a coward. Remember how Farmer Brown's boy saved you from Shadow the Weasel. Come on! Dee, dee, dee, come on!" With that Tommy flew across to the tree close by the house.

Happy Jack scrambled up on the old stone wall and looked this way and looked that way. He couldn't see a thing to be afraid of. He jumped down and ran a few steps. Then his heart failed, and he scampered back to the old stone wall in a panic. After a few minutes he tried again, and once more a foolish fear sent him back. The third time he gritted his teeth, said to himself over and over, "I will! I will! I will!" and ran with all his might. In no time at all he was across the dooryard and up in the big tree, his heart pounding with excitement.

"Dee, dee, dee," called Tommy Tit.

Happy Jack looked over to the house, and there sat Tommy on a window-sill, helping himself to the most delicious-looking cracked nuts. The sight of them made Happy Jack's mouth water. A long branch hung down over the window and almost touched the sill. Happy Jack ventured half way and stopped. Somehow it seemed very dangerous to go so close to that window.

"Come on! Come on! What are you afraid of?" called Tommy.

Something like shame that such a little fellow as Tommy Tit should dare to go where he did not, crept into Happy Jack's heart. With a quick little run and jump he was on the sill, and a second later he was staring in at all the strange things inside. At first he didn't see anything of Farmer Brown's boy, but in a few minutes he made him out. He was lying down all covered over except his head. There *was* something the matter with him. Happy Jack didn't need to be told that, and a great pity filled his heart. He wanted to do something for Farmer Brown's boy.

XX
What Was the Matter with Farmer Brown's Boy?

He who climbs the highest has the farthest to fall, but often it is worth the risk.

Happy Jack.

All the way home from his visit to Farmer Brown's house Happy Jack Squirrel puzzled and wondered over what he had seen. He had peeped in at a window and seen Farmer Brown's boy lying all covered up, with only his head showing. Happy Jack couldn't see very well, but somehow that head didn't look just right. One thing was sure, and that was there was something wrong with Farmer Brown's boy. He never would have been lying still like that if there hadn't been.

Happy Jack had been so troubled by what he saw that he had hardly tasted the nuts he had found on the window-sill. "I am going to make him another call to-morrow," said he when he and Tommy Tit were once more back in the Green Forest.

"Of course," replied Tommy. "I expected you would. I will be around for you at the same time.

You're not afraid any more to go up there, are you?"

"No-o," replied Happy Jack, slowly. The truth is, he was still a little afraid. It seemed to him a terribly venturesome thing to cross that open dooryard, but having done it once in safety, he knew that it would be easier the next time. It was. The next morning he and Tommy Tit went just as before, and this time Happy Jack scampered across the dooryard the very first time he tried. They found things just as they had been the day before. They saw Farmer Brown's boy, but he didn't see them. Tommy Tit was just going to tap on the window to let him know they were there, when a door inside opened, and in walked Mrs. Brown. It frightened them so that Tommy Tit flew away without tasting a single nut, and Happy Jack nearly fell as he scrambled back into the tree close by the window. You see, they never had made her acquaintance, and having her walk in so suddenly frightened them terribly. They didn't stop to think that there was nothing to fear because there was the window between. Somehow they couldn't understand that queer stuff that they could see through but which shut them out. If they had seen Mrs. Brown go to the window and put more cracked nuts on the sill, perhaps they would have been less afraid. But they had been too badly frightened to look back, and so they didn't know anything about that.

The next morning Tommy Tit was on hand as usual, but he found Happy Jack a little doubtful about paying another visit. He wasn't wholly over his scare of the day before. It took him some time to make up his mind to go, but finally he did. This time when they reached the tree close by the house, they found a great surprise awaiting them. Farmer Brown's boy was sitting just inside the window, looking out. At least, they thought it was Farmer Brown's boy, but when they got a little nearer, they grew doubtful. It looked like Farmer Brown's boy, and yet it didn't. His cheeks stuck way out just as Striped Chipmunk's do when he has them stuffed full of corn or nuts.

Happy Jack stared at him very hard. "My goodness, I didn't know he carried his food that way!" he exclaimed. "I should think it would be dreadfully uncomfortable."

If Farmer Brown's boy could have heard that, he certainly would have tried to laugh, and if he had—well, it was bad enough when he tried to smile at the sight of Tommy Tit and Happy Jack. He didn't smile at all but made up an awful face instead and clapped both hands to his cheeks. Happy Jack and Tommy Tit didn't know what to make of it, and it was some time before they made up their minds that it really was Farmer Brown's boy, and that they had nothing to fear. But when they finally ventured on to the sill and, as they helped themselves to nuts, saw the smile in his eyes, though he did not smile with his mouth at all, they knew that it was he, and that he was glad that they had called. Then they were glad too.

But what was the matter with Farmer Brown's boy? Happy Jack puzzled over it all the rest of the day, and then gave it up.

XXI
Happy Jack Squirrel Grows Very Bold

When you find a friend in trouble
  Pass along a word of cheer.
Often it is very helpful
  Just to feel a friend is near.

Happy Jack.

Every day Happy Jack visited the window sill of Farmer Brown's house to call on Farmer Brown's boy, who was always waiting for him just inside the window. In fact Happy Jack had got into the habit of getting his breakfast there, for always there were fat, delicious nuts on the window-sill, and it was much easier and more comfortable to breakfast there than to hunt up his own hidden supplies and perhaps have to dig down through the snow to get them. Most people are just like Happy Jack—they do the easiest thing.

Each day Farmer Brown's boy looked more and more like himself. His cheeks stuck out less and less, and finally did not stick out at all. And now he smiled at Happy Jack with his mouth as well as with his eyes. You know when his cheeks had stuck out so, he couldn't smile at all except with his eyes. Happy Jack didn't know what had been the matter with Farmer Brown's boy, but whatever it was, he was better now, and that made Happy Jack feel better.

One morning he got a surprise. When he ran out along the branch of the tree that led to the window-sill he suddenly discovered something wrong. There were no nuts on the sill! More than this there was something very suspicious looking about the window. It didn't look just right. The truth is it was partly open, but Happy Jack didn't understand this, not then, anyway. He stopped short and scolded, a way he has when things don't suit him. Farmer Brown's boy came to the window and called to him. Then he thrust a hand out, and in it were some of the fattest nuts Happy Jack ever had seen. His mouth watered right away. There might be something wrong with the window, but certainly the sill was all right. It would do no harm to go that far.

So Happy Jack nimbly jumped across to the window-sill. Farmer Brown's boy's hand with the fat nuts was still there, and Happy Jack lost no time in getting one. Then he sat up on the sill to eat it. My, but it was good! It was just as good as it had looked. Happy Jack's eyes twinkled as he ate. When he had finished that nut, he wanted another. But now Farmer Brown's boy had drawn his hand inside the window. He was still holding it out with the nuts in it, but to get them Happy Jack must go inside, and he couldn't get it out of his head that

that was a very dangerous thing to do. What if that window should be closed while he was in there? Then he would be a prisoner.

So he sat up and begged. He knew that Farmer Brown's boy knew what he wanted. But Farmer Brown's boy kept his hand just where it was.

"Come on, you little rascal," said he. "You ought to know me well enough by this time to know that I won't hurt you or let any harm come to you. Hurry up, because I can't stand here all day. You see, I've just got over the mumps, and if I should catch cold I might be sick again. Come along now, and show how brave you are."

Of course Happy Jack couldn't understand what he said. If he could have, he might have guessed that it was the mumps that had made Farmer Brown's boy look so like Striped Chipmunk when he has his cheeks stuffed with nuts. But if he couldn't understand what Farmer Brown's boy said, he had no difficulty in understanding that if he wanted those nuts he would have to go after them. So at last he screwed up his courage and put his head inside. Nothing happened, so he went wholly in and sat on the inside sill. Then by reaching out as far as he could without tumbling off, he managed to get one of those nuts, and as soon as he had it, he dodged outside to eat it.

Farmer Brown's boy laughed, and putting the rest of the nuts outside, he closed the window. Happy Jack ate his fill and then scampered back to the Green Forest. He felt all puffed up with pride. He felt that he had been very, very bold, and he was anxious to tell Tommy Tit the Chickadee, who had not been with him that morning, how bold he had been.

"Pooh, that's nothing!" replied Tommy, when he had heard about it. "I've done that often."

XXII
Happy Jack Dares Tommy Tit

A wise philosopher is he
Who takes things as they chance to be,
And in them sees that which is best
While trying to forget the rest.

Happy Jack.

Somehow Happy Jack's day had been spoiled. He knew that he had no business to allow it to be spoiled, but it was, just the same. You see, he had been all puffed up with pride because he thought himself a very bold fellow because he had really been inside Farmer Brown's house. He couldn't help feeling quite puffed up about it. But when he told Tommy Tit the Chickadee about it, Tommy had said, "Pooh! I've done that often."

That was what had spoiled the day for Happy Jack. He knew that if Tommy Tit said that he had done a thing, he had, for Tommy always tells the truth and nothing but the truth. So Happy Jack hadn't been so dreadfully bold, after all, and had nothing to brag about. It made him feel quite put out. He actually tried to make himself feel that it was all the fault of Tommy Tit, and that he wanted to get even with him. He thought about it all the rest of the day, and just before he fell asleep that night an idea came to him.

"I know what I'll do! I'll dare Tommy to go as far inside Farmer Brown's house as I do!" he exclaimed, and went to sleep to dream that he was the boldest, bravest squirrel that ever lived.

The next morning when he reached the tree close by Farmer Brown's house, he found Tommy Tit already there, flitting about impatiently and calling his loudest, which wasn't very loud, for you know Tommy is a very little fellow, and his voice is not very loud. But he was doing his best to call Farmer Brown's boy. You see, there wasn't a single nut on the window-sill, and the window was closed. Pretty soon Farmer Brown's boy came to the window and opened it. But he didn't put out any nuts. Tommy Tit at once flew over to the sill, and to show that he was just as bold, Happy Jack followed. Looking inside, they saw Farmer Brown's boy standing in the middle of the room, holding out a dish of nuts and smiling at them. This was the chance Happy Jack wanted to try the plan he had thought of the night before.

"I dare you to go way in there and get a nut," said he to Tommy Tit. He hoped that Tommy would be afraid.

But Tommy wasn't anything of the kind. "Dee, dee, dee! Come on!" he cried, and flitted over and helped himself to a cracked nut and was back with it before Happy Jack could make up his mind to jump down inside. Of course now that he had dared Tommy Tit, and Tommy had taken the dare, he just had to do it too. It looked a long way in to where Farmer Brown's boy was standing. Twice he started and turned back. Then he heard Tommy Tit chuckle. That was too much. He wouldn't be laughed at. He just wouldn't. He scampered across, grabbed a nut, and rushed back to the window-sill, where he ate the nut. It was easier to go after the second nut, and when he went for the third, he had made up his mind that it was perfectly safe in there, and so he sat up on a chair and ate it. Presently he felt quite at home, and when he had eaten all the nuts he wanted, he ran all around the room, examining all the strange things there.

This was a little more than Tommy Tit could make up his mind to do. He wasn't afraid to fly in for a nut and then fly out again, but he couldn't feel easy inside a house like that. Of course, this made Happy Jack feel good all over. You see, he felt that now he really did have something to boast about. No one else in all the Green Forest or on the Green Meadows could say that they had been all over Farmer Brown's boy's room as he had. Happy Jack swelled himself out at the thought. Now everybody would say, "What a bold fellow!"

XXIII
Sammy Jay Is Quite Upset

I know of nothing sweeter than
Success to Squirrel or to man.

Happy Jack.

Very few people can be all puffed up with pride without showing it. Happy Jack Squirrel couldn't. Just to have looked at him you would have known that he was feeling very, very good about something. When he thought no one was looking, he would actually strut. And it was all because he considered himself a very bold fellow. That was a new feeling for Happy Jack. He knew that all his neighbors considered him rather timid, and many a time he had envied, actually envied Jimmy Skunk and Reddy Fox and Unc' Billy Possum and even Sammy Jay because they did such bold things and had dared to visit Farmer Brown's dooryard and henhouse in spite of Bowser the Hound.

But now he felt that he dared do a thing that not one of them dared do. He dared go right into Farmer Brown's house and make himself quite at home in the room of Farmer Brown's boy. He felt that he was a tremendously brave fellow. You see, he quite forgot one thing. He forgot that he had found out that love destroys fear, and that though it might look to others like a very bold thing to walk right into Farmer Brown's house, it really wasn't bold at all, because all the time he *knew* that no harm would come to him. It is never brave to do a thing that you are not afraid to do. It had been brave of him to go in at that open window the first time, because then he had been afraid, but now he wasn't afraid, and so it was no longer either brave or bold of him.

Tommy Tit the Chickadee knew all this, and he used to chuckle to himself as he saw how proud of himself Happy Jack was, but he said nothing to any one about it. Of course, it wasn't long before some others began to notice Happy Jack's pride. One of the first was Sammy Jay. There is very little that escapes Sammy Jay's sharp eyes. Silently stealing through the Green Forest early one morning, he surprised Happy Jack strutting.

"Huh," said he, "what are you feeling so big about?"

Like a flash the thought came to Happy Jack that here was a chance to show what a bold fellow he had become. "Hello, Sammy!" he exclaimed. "Are you feeling very brave this morning?"

"Me feeling brave? What are you talking about? If I was as timid as you are, I wouldn't ever talk about bravery to other people. If there is anything you dare to do that I don't, I've never heard of it," retorted Sammy Jay.

"Come on!" cried Happy Jack. "I'm going to get my.breakfast, and I dare you to follow me!"

Sammy Jay actually laughed right out. "Go ahead. Wherever you go, I'll go," he declared.

Happy Jack started right away for Farmer Brown's house, and Sammy followed. Through the Old Orchard, across the dooryard and into the big maple tree Happy Jack led the way, and Sammy followed, all the time wondering what was up. He had been there many times. In fact, he had had many a good meal of suet there during the cold weather, for Farmer Brown's boy had kept a big piece tied to a branch of the maple tree for those who were hungry.

Sammy was a little surprised when he saw Happy Jack jump over on to the window-sill. Still, he had been on that window-sill more than once himself, when he had made sure that no one was near, and had helped himself to the cracked nuts he had found there.

"Come on!" called Happy Jack, his eyes twinkling.

Sammy Jay chuckled. "He thinks I don't dare go over there," he thought. "Well, I'll fool him."

With a hasty look to see that no danger was near, he spread his wings to follow Happy Jack on to the window-sill. Happy Jack waited to make sure that he really was coming and then slipped in at the open window and scampered over to a table on the farther side of the room and helped himself from a dish of nuts there.

When Sammy saw Happy Jack disappear inside he gave a little gasp. When he looked inside and saw Happy Jack making himself quite at home, he gasped again. And when he saw a door open and Farmer Brown's boy enter, and still Happy Jack did not run, he was too upset for words. He didn't dare stay to see more, and for once in his life was quite speechless as he flew back to the Green Forest.

XXIV
A Dream Comes True

What are all our dreams made up of
  That they often are so queer?
Wishes, hopes, and fond desires
  All mixed up with foolish fears.

Happy Jack.

Which is worse, to have a very beautiful dream never come true, or to have a bad dream really come true? Happy Jack Squirrel says the latter is worse, much worse. Dreams do come true once in a great while, you know. One of Happy Jack's did. It came true, and it made a great difference in Happy Jack's life. You see, it was like this:

Happy Jack had had so many things to think of that he had almost forgotten about Shadow the Weasel. Happy Jack hadn't seen or heard anything of him since Farmer Brown's boy had chased him into the Green Forest and so saved Happy Jack's life. Since then life had been too full of pleasant things to think of anything so unpleasant as Shadow the Weasel. But one night Happy Jack had a bad dream. Yes, Sir, it was a very bad dream. He dreamed that once more Shadow the Weasel was after him, and this time there was no Farmer

Brown's boy to run to for help. Shadow was right at his heels and in one more jump would have him. Happy Jack opened his mouth to scream, and—awoke.

He was all ashake with fright. It was a great relief to find that it was only a dream, but even then he couldn't get over it right away. He was glad that it was almost morning, and just as soon as it was light enough to see, he crept out. It was too early to go over to Farmer Brown's house; Farmer Brown's boy wouldn't be up yet. So Happy Jack ran over to one of his favorite lookouts, a tall chestnut tree, and there, with his back against the trunk, high above the ground, he watched the Green Forest wake as the first Sunbeams stole through it. But all the time he kept thinking of that dreadful dream.

A little spot of black moving against the white snow caught his sharp eyes. What was it? He leaned forward and held his breath, as he tried to make sure. Ah, now he could see! Just ahead of that black thing was a long, slim fellow all in white, and that black spot was his tail. If it hadn't been for that, Happy Jack very likely wouldn't have seen him at all. It was Shadow the Weasel! He was running swiftly, first to one side and then to the other, with his nose to the snow. He was hunting. There was no doubt about that. He was hunting for his breakfast.

Happy Jack's eyes grew wide with fear. Would

Shadow find his tracks? It looked very much as if Shadow was heading for Happy Jack's house, and Happy Jack was glad, very glad, that that bad dream had waked him and made him so uneasy that he had come out. Otherwise he might have been caught right in his own bed. Shadow was almost at Happy Jack's house when he stopped abruptly with his nose to the snow and sniffed eagerly. Then he turned, and with his nose to the snow, started straight toward the tree where Happy Jack was. Happy Jack waited to see no more. He knew now that Shadow had found his trail and that it was to be a case of run for his life.

"My dream has come true!" he sobbed as he ran. "My dream has come true, and I don't know what to do!" But all the time he kept on running as fast as ever he could, which really was the only thing to do.

XXV
Happy Jack Has a Happy Thought

Who runs when danger comes his way
Will live to run some other day.
Happy Jack.

Frightened and breathless, running with all his might from Shadow the Weasel, Happy Jack Squirrel was in despair. He didn't know what to do or where to go. The last time he had run from Shadow he had run to Farmer Brown's boy, who had just happened to be near, and Farmer Brown's boy had chased Shadow the Weasel away. But now it was too early in the morning for him to expect to meet Farmer Brown's boy. In fact, jolly, round, Red Mr. Sun had hardly kicked his bedclothes off yet, and Happy Jack was very sure that Farmer Brown's boy was still asleep.

Now most of us are creatures of habit. We do the thing that we have been in the habit of doing, and do it without thinking anything about it. That is why good habits are such a blessing. Happy Jack Squirrel is just like the rest of us. He has habits, both good and bad. Of late, he had been in the habit of getting his breakfast at Farmer Brown's house every morning, so now when he began to run from Shadow the Weasel he just naturally ran in the direction of Farmer Brown's house from force of habit. In fact, he was halfway there before he realized in which direction he was running.

Right then a thought came to him. It gave him a wee bit of hope, and seemed to help him run just a little faster. If the window of Farmer Brown's boy's room was open, he would run in there, and perhaps Shadow the Weasel wouldn't dare follow! How he did hope that that window would be open! He knew that it was his only chance. He wasn't quite sure that it really was a chance, for Shadow was such a bold fellow that he might not be afraid to follow him right in, but it was worth trying.

Along the stone wall beside the Old Orchard raced Happy Jack to the dooryard of Farmer Brown, and after him ran Shadow the Weasel, and Shadow looked as if he was enjoying himself. No doubt he was. He knew just as well as Happy Jack did that there was small chance of meeting Farmer Brown's boy so early in the morning, so he felt very sure how that chase was going to end, and that when it did end he would breakfast on Squirrel.

By the time Happy Jack reached the dooryard, Shadow was only a few jumps behind him, and Happy Jack was pretty well out of breath. He didn't stop to look to see if the way was clear. There wasn't time for that. Besides, there could be no greater danger in front than was almost at his heels, and so, without looking one way or another, he scampered across the dooryard and up the big maple tree close to the house. Shadow the Weasel was surprised. He had not dreamed that Happy Jack would come over here. But Shadow is a bold fellow, and it made little difference to him where Happy Jack went. At least, that is what he thought.

So he followed Happy Jack across the dooryard and up the maple tree. He took his time about it, for he knew by the way Happy Jack had run that he was pretty nearly at the end of his strength. "He never'll get out of this tree," thought Shadow, as he started to climb it. He fully expected to find Happy Jack huddled in a miserable little heap somewhere near the top. Just imagine how surprised he was when he discovered that Happy Jack wasn't to be seen. He rubbed his angry little red eyes, and they grew angrier and redder than before.

"Must be a hollow up here somewhere," he muttered. "I'll just follow the scent of his feet, and that will lead me to him."

But when that scent led him out on a branch the tip of which brushed against Farmer Brown's house Shadow got another surprise. There was no sign of Happy Jack. He couldn't have reached the roof. There was no place he could have gone unless——. Shadow stared across at a window open about two inches.

"He couldn't have!" muttered Shadow. "He wouldn't dare. He couldn't have!"

But Happy Jack had. He had gone inside that window.

XXVI
Farmer Brown's Boy Wakes with a Start

Never think another crazy just because it happens you
Never've heard of just the thing that they have started
out to do.

Happy Jack.

Isn't it queer how hard it seems to be for some boys to go to bed at the proper time and how much harder it is for them to get up in the morning? It was just so with Farmer Brown's boy. I suppose he wouldn't have been a real boy if it hadn't been so. Of course, while he was sick with the mumps, he didn't have to get up, and while he was getting over the mumps his mother let him sleep as long as he wanted to in the morning. That was very nice, but it made it all the harder to get up when he should after he was well again. In summer it wasn't so bad getting up early, but in winter—well, that was the one thing about winter that Farmer Brown's boy didn't like.

On this particular morning Farmer Brown had called him, and he had replied with a sleepy "All right," and then had rolled over and promptly gone to sleep again. In two minutes he was dreaming just as if there were no such things as duties to be done. For a while they were very pleasant dreams, very pleasant indeed. But suddenly they changed. A terrible monster was chasing him. It had great red eyes as big as saucers, and sparks of fire flew from its mouth. It had great claws as big as ice tongs, and it roared like a lion. In his dream Farmer Brown's boy was running with all his might. Then he tripped and fell, and somehow he couldn't get up again. The terrible monster came nearer and nearer. Farmer Brown's boy tried to scream and couldn't. He was so frightened that he had lost his voice. The terrible monster was right over him now and reached out one of his huge paws with the great claws. One of them touched him on the cheek, and it burned like fire.

With a yell, a real, genuine yell, Farmer Brown's boy awoke and sprang out of bed. For a minute he couldn't think where he was. Then with a sigh of relief he realized that he was safe in his own snug little room with the first Jolly Little Sunbeam creeping in at the window to wish him good morning and chide him for being such a lazy fellow. A thump and a scurry of little feet caught his attention, and he turned to see a Gray Squirrel running for the open window. It jumped up on the sill, looked out, then jumped down inside again, and ran over to a corner of the room, where he crouched as if in great fear. It was clear that he had been badly frightened by the yell of Farmer Brown's boy, and that he was still more frightened by something he had seen when he looked out of the window.

A great light broke over Farmer Brown's boy. "Happy Jack, you little rascal, I believe you are the terrible monster that scared me so!" he exclaimed. "I believe you were on my bed, and that it was your claws that I felt on my face. But what ails you? You look frightened almost to death."

He went over to the window and looked out. A movement in the big maple tree just outside caught his attention. He saw a long, slim white form dart down the tree and disappear. He knew who it was. It was Shadow the Weasel.

"So that pesky Weasel has been after you again, and you came to me for help," said he gently, as he coaxed Happy Jack to come to him. "This is the place to come to every time. Poor little chap, you're all of a tremble. I guess I know how you feel when a Weasel is after you. I guess you feel just as I felt when I dreamed that that monster was after me. My, but you certainly did give me a scare when you touched my face!" He gently stroked Happy Jack as he talked, and Happy Jack let him.

"Breakfast!" called a voice from downstairs.

"Coming!" replied Farmer Brown's boy as he put Happy Jack on the table by a dish of nuts and began to scramble into his clothes.

XXVII
Happy Jack Is Afraid to Go Home

Safety first is the best rule to insure a long life.
Happy Jack.

Happy Jack didn't dare go home. Can you think of anything more dreadful than to be afraid to go to your own home? Why, home is the dearest place in the world, and it should be the safest. Just think how you would feel if you should be away from home, and then you should learn that it wouldn't be safe for you to go back there again, and you had no other place to go. If often happens that way with the little people of the Green Meadows and the Green Forest. It was that way with Happy Jack Squirrel now.

You see, Happy Jack knew that Shadow the Weasel is not one to give up easily. Shadow has one very good trait, and that is persistence. He is not easily discouraged. When he sets out to do a thing, usually he does it. If he starts to get a thing, usually he gets it. No, he isn't easily discouraged. Happy Jack knows this. No one knows it better. So Happy Jack didn't dare to go home. He knew that any minute of night or day Shadow might surprise him there, and that would be the end of him. He more than half suspected that Shadow was at that very time hiding somewhere along the way ready to spring out on him if he should try to go back home.

He had stayed in the room of Farmer Brown's boy until Mrs. Brown had come to make the bed. Then he had jumped out the window into the big maple tree. He wasn't quite sure of Mrs. Brown yet. She had kindly eyes. They were just like the eyes of Farmer Brown's boy. But he didn't feel really acquainted yet, and he felt safer outside than inside the room while she was there.

> "Oh dear, oh dear! What shall I do?
> I have no home, and so
> To keep me warm and snug and safe
> I have no place to go!"

Happy Jack said this over and over as he sat in the maple tree, trying to decide what was to be done.

"I wonder what ails that Squirrel. He seems to be doing a lot of scolding," said Mrs. Brown, as she looked out of the window. And that shows how easy it is to misunderstand people when we don't know all about their affairs. Mrs. Brown thought that Happy Jack was scolding, when all the time he was just frightened and worried and wondering where he could go and what he could do to feel safe from Shadow the Weasel.

Because he didn't dare to go back to the Green Forest, he spent most of the day in the big maple tree close to Farmer Brown's house. The window had been closed, so he couldn't go inside. He looked at it longingly a great many times during the day, hoping that he would find it open. But he didn't. You see, it was opened only at night when Farmer Brown's boy went to bed, so that he would have plenty of fresh air all night. Of course Happy Jack didn't know that. All his life he had had plenty of fresh air all the time, and he couldn't understand how people could live in houses all shut up.

Late that afternoon Farmer Brown's boy, who had been at school all day, came whistling into the yard. He noticed Happy Jack right away. "Hello! You back again! Isn't one good meal a day enough?" he exclaimed.

"He's been there all day," said his mother, who had come to the door just in time to overhear him. "I don't know what ails him."

Then Farmer Brown's boy noticed how forlorn Happy Jack looked. He remembered Happy Jack's fright that morning.

"I know what's the matter!" he cried. "It's that Weasel. The poor little chap is afraid to go home. We must see what we can do for him. I wonder if he will stay if I make a new house for him. I believe I'll try it and see."

XXVIII
Happy Jack Finds a New Home

They say the very darkest clouds
  Are lined with silver bright and fair,
Though how they know I do not see,
  And neither do I really care.
It's good to believe, and so I try
  To believe 'tis true with all my might,
That nothing is so seeming dark
  But has a hidden side that's bright.

Happy Jack.

Certainly things couldn't look much darker than they did to Happy Jack Squirrel as he sat in the big maple tree at the side of Farmer Brown's house, and saw jolly, round, red Mr. Sun getting ready to go to bed behind the Purple Hills. He was afraid to go to his home in the Green Forest because Shadow the Weasel might be waiting for him there. He was afraid of the night which would soon come. He was cold, and he was hungry. Altogether he was as miserable a little Squirrel as ever was seen.

He had just made up his mind that he would have to go look for a hollow in one of the trees in the Old Orchard in which to spend the night, when around the corner of the house came Farmer

Brown's boy with something under one arm and dragging a ladder. He whistled cheerily to Happy Jack as he put the ladder against the tree and climbed up. By this time Happy Jack had grown so timid that he was just a little afraid of Farmer Brown's boy, so he climbed as high up in the tree as he could get and watched what was going on below. Even if he was afraid, there was comfort in having Farmer Brown's boy near.

For some time Farmer Brown's boy worked busily at the place where the branch that Happy Jack knew so well started out from the trunk of the tree towards the window of Farmer Brown's boy's room. When he had fixed things to suit him, he went down the ladder and carried it away with him. In the crotch of the tree he had left the queer thing that he had brought under his arm. In spite of his fears, Happy Jack was curious. Little by little he crept nearer. What he saw was a box with a round hole, just about big enough for him to go through, in one end, and in front of it a little shelf. On the shelf were some of the nuts that he liked best.

For a long time Happy Jack looked and looked. Was it a trap? Somehow he couldn't believe that it was. What would Farmer Brown's boy try to trap him for when they were such good friends? At last the sight of the nuts was too much for him. It certainly was safe enough to help himself to those. How good they tasted! Almost before he knew it, they were gone. Then he got up courage enough to peep inside. The box was filled with soft hay. It certainly did look inviting in there to a fellow who had no home and no place to go. He put his head inside. Finally he went wholly in. It was just as nice as it looked.

"I believe," thought Happy Jack, "that he made this little house just for me, and that he put all this hay in here for my bed. He doesn't know much about making a bed, but I guess he means well."

With that he went to work happily to make up a bed to suit him, and by the time the first Black Shadow had crept as far as the big maple tree, Happy Jack was curled up fast asleep in his new house.

XXIX
Farmer Brown's Boy Takes a Prisoner

The craftiest and cleverest, the strongest and the bold
Will make mistakes like other folks, young, middle-
aged, and old.

Happy Jack.

Happy Jack Squirrel was happy once more. He liked his new house, the house that Farmer Brown's boy had made for him and fastened in the big maple tree close by the house in which he himself lived. Happy Jack and Farmer Brown's boy were getting to be greater friends than ever. Every morning Happy Jack jumped over to the window-sill and then in at the open window of the room of Farmer Brown's boy. There he was sure to find a good breakfast of fat hickory nuts. When Farmer Brown's boy overslept, as he did sometimes, Happy Jack would jump up on the bed and waken him. He thought this great fun. So did Farmer Brown's boy, though sometimes when he was very sleepy he pretended to scold, especially on Sunday mornings when he did not have to get up as early as on other days.

Of course, Black Pussy had soon discovered that Happy Jack was living in the big maple tree, and she spent a great deal of time sitting at the foot of it and glaring up at him with a hungry look in her eyes, although she wasn't hungry at all, for she had plenty to eat. Several times she climbed up in the tree and tried to catch him. At first he had been afraid, but he soon found out that Black Pussy was not at all at home in a tree as he was. After that, he rather enjoyed having her try to catch him. It was almost like a game. It was great fun to scold at her and let her get very near him and then, just as she was sure that she was going to catch him, to jump out of her reach. After a while she was content to sit at the foot of the tree and just glare at him.

Happy Jack had only one worry now, and this didn't trouble him a great deal. It was possible that Shadow the Weasel might take it into his head to try to surprise him some night. Happy Jack knew that by this time Shadow must know where he was living, for of course Sammy Jay had found out, and Sammy is one of those who tells all he knows. Still, being so close to Farmer Brown's boy gave Happy Jack a very comfortable feeling.

Now all this time Farmer Brown's boy had not forgotten Shadow the Weasel and how he had driven Happy Jack out of the Green Forest, and he had wondered a great many times if it wouldn't be a kindness to the other little people if he should trap Shadow and put him out of the way. But you know he had given up trapping, and somehow he didn't like to think of setting a trap, even for such a mischief-maker as Shadow. Then something happened that made Farmer Brown's boy very, very angry. One morning, when he went to feed the biddies, he found that Shadow had visited the henhouse in the night and killed three of his best pullets. That decided him. He felt sure that Shadow would come again, and he meant to give Shadow a surprise. He hunted until he found the little hole through which Shadow had got into the henhouse, and there he set a trap.

"I don't like to do it, but I've got to," said he. "If he had been content with one, it would have been bad enough, but he killed three just from the love of killing, and it is high time that something be done to get rid of him."

The very next morning Happy Jack saw Farmer Brown's boy coming from the henhouse with something under his arm. He came straight over to the foot of the big maple tree and put the thing he was carrying down on the ground. He whistled to Happy Jack, and as Happy Jack came down to see what it was all about, Farmer Brown's boy grinned. "Here's a friend of yours you probably will be glad to see," said he.

At first, all Happy Jack could make out was a kind of wire box. Then he saw something white inside, and it moved. Very suspiciously Happy Jack came nearer. Then his heart gave a great leap. That wire box was a cage, and glaring between the wires with red, angry eyes was Shadow the Weasel! He was a prisoner! Right away Happy Jack was so excited that he acted as if he were crazy. He no longer had a single thing to be afraid of. Do you wonder that he was excited?

XXX
A Prisoner without Fear

A bad name is easy to get but hard to live down.
Happy Jack.

Shadow the Weasel was a prisoner. He who always had been free to go and come as he pleased and to do as he pleased was now in a little narrow cage and quite helpless. For once he had been careless, and this was the result. Farmer Brown's boy had caught him in a trap. Of course, he should have known better than to have visited the henhouse a second time after killing three of the best pullets there. He should have known that Farmer Brown's boy would be sure to do something about it. The truth is, he had yielded to temptation when common sense had warned him not to. So he had no one to blame for his present difficulty but himself, and he knew it.

At first he had been in a terrible rage and had bitten at the wires until he had made his mouth sore. When he had made sure that the wires were stouter than his teeth, he wisely stopped trying to get out in that way, and made up his mind that the only thing to do was to watch for a chance to slip out, if the door of the cage should happen to be left unfastened.

Of course it hurt his pride terribly to be made fun of by those who always had feared him. Happy Jack Squirrel was the first one of these to see him. Farmer Brown's boy had put the cage down near the foot of the big maple tree in which Happy Jack was living, because Shadow had driven him out of the Green Forest. As soon as Happy Jack had made sure that Shadow really and truly was a prisoner and so quite harmless, he had acted as if he were crazy. Perhaps he was—crazy with joy. You see, he no longer had anything to be really afraid of, for there was no one but Shadow from whom he could not get away by running into his house. Billy Mink was the only other one who could follow him there, and Billy was not likely to come climbing up a tree so close to Farmer Brown's house.

So Happy Jack raced up and down the tree in the very greatest excitement, and his tongue went quite as fast as his legs. He wanted everybody to know that Shadow was a prisoner at last. At first he did not dare go very close to the cage. You see, he had so long feared Shadow that he was still afraid of him even though he was so helpless. But little by little Happy Jack grew bolder and came very close. And then he began doing something not at all nice. He began calling Shadow names and making fun of him, and telling him how he wasn't afraid of him. It was all very foolish and worse—it was like hitting a foe who was helpless.

Of course Happy Jack hastened to tell

It wasn't long before Shadow began to receive many visitors. *See page 98.*

everybody he met all about Shadow, so it wasn't long before Shadow began to receive many visitors. Whenever Farmer Brown's boy was not around there was sure to be one or more of the little people who had feared Shadow to taunt him and make fun of him. Somehow it seems as if always it is that way when people get into trouble. You know it is very easy to appear to be bold and brave when there is nothing to be afraid of. Of course that isn't bravery at all, though many seem to think it is.

Now what do you think that right down in their hearts all these little people who came to jeer at Shadow the Weasel hoped they would see? Why, they hoped they would see Shadow afraid. Yes, Sir, that is just what they hoped. But they didn't. That is where they were disappointed. Not once did Shadow show the least sign of fear. He didn't know what Farmer Brown's boy would do with him, and he had every reason to fear that if he was not to be kept a prisoner for the rest of his natural life, something dreadful would be the end. But he was too proud and too brave to let any one know that any such fear ever entered his mind. Whatever his faults, Shadow is no coward. He boldly took bits of meat which Farmer Brown's boy brought to him, and not once appeared in the least afraid, so that, much as he disliked him, Farmer Brown's boy actually had to admire him. He was a prisoner, but he kept just as stout a heart as ever.

XXXI
What Farmer Brown's Boy Did with Shadow

Ribble, dibble, dibble, dab!
Some people have the gift of gab!
Some people have no tongues at all
To trip them up and make them fall.
Happy Jack.

It is a fact, one of the biggest facts in all the world, that tongues make the greatest part of all the trouble that brings uncomfortable feelings, and bitterness and sadness and suffering and sorrow. If it wasn't for unruly, careless, mean tongues, the Great World would be a million times better to live in, a million times happier. It is because of his unruly tongue that Sammy Jay is forever getting into trouble. It is the same way with Chatterer the Red Squirrel. And it is just the same way with a great many little boys and girls, and with grown-ups as well.

When the little people of the Green Forest and Green Meadows who fear Shadow the Weasel found that he was a prisoner, many of them took particular pains to visit him when the way was clear, just to make fun of him and tease him and tell him that they were not afraid of him and that they were glad that he was a prisoner, and that they were sure something dreadful would happen to him and they hoped it would. Shadow said never a word in reply. He was too wise to do that. He just turned his back on them. But all the time he was storing up in his mind all these hateful things, and he meant, if ever he got free again, to make life very uncomfortable for those whose foolish tongues were trying to make him more miserable than he already felt.

But these little people with the foolish tongues didn't stop to think of what might happen. They just took it for granted that Shadow never again would run wild and free in the Green Forest, and so they just let their tongues run and enjoyed doing it. Perhaps they wouldn't have, if they could have known just what was going on in the mind of Farmer Brown's boy. Ever since he had found Shadow in the trap which he had set for him in the henhouse, Farmer Brown's boy had been puzzling over what he should do with his prisoner. At first he had thought he would keep him in a cage the rest of his life. But somehow, whenever he looked into Shadow's fierce little eyes and saw how unafraid they looked, he got to thinking of how terrible it must be to be shut up in a little narrow cage when one has had all the Green Forest in which to go and come. Then he thought that he would kill Shadow and put him out of his misery at once.

"He killed my pullets, and he is always hunting the harmless little people of the Green Forest and the Green Meadows, so he deserves to be killed," thought Farmer Brown's boy. "He's a pest."

Then he remembered that after all Shadow was one of Old Mother Nature's little people, and that he must serve some purpose in Mother Nature's great plan. Bad as he seemed, she must have some use for him. Perhaps it was to teach others through fear of him how to be smarter and take better care of themselves and so be better fitted to do their parts. The more he thought of this, the harder it was for Farmer Brown's boy to make up his mind to kill him. But if he couldn't keep him a prisoner and he couldn't kill him, what could he do?

He was scowling down at Shadow one morning and puzzling over this when a happy idea came to him. "I know what I'll do!" he exclaimed. Without another word he picked up the cage with Shadow in it and started off across the Green Meadows, which now, you know, were not green at all but covered with snow. Happy Jack watched him out of sight. He had gone in the direction of the Old Pasture. He was gone a long time, and when he did return the cage was empty.

Happy Jack blinked at the empty cage. Then he began to ask in a scolding tone, "What did you do with him? What did you do with him?"

Farmer Brown's boy just smiled and tossed a nut to Happy Jack. And far up in the Old Pasture, Shadow the Weasel was once more free. It was well for Happy Jack's peace of mind that he didn't know that.

XXXII
Happy Jack Is Perfectly Happy

Never say a thing is so
Unless you absolutely know.
Just remember every day
To be quite sure of what you say.

Happy Jack.

Taking things for granted doesn't do at all in this world. To take a thing for granted is to think that it is so without taking the trouble to find out whether it is or not. It is apt not only to get you yourself into trouble, but to make trouble for other people as well. Happy Jack saw Farmer Brown's boy carry Shadow the Weasel away in a cage, and he saw him bring back the cage empty. What could he have done with Shadow? For a while he teased Farmer Brown's boy to tell him, but of course Farmer Brown's boy didn't understand Happy Jack's language.

Now Happy Jack knew just what he would like to believe. He would like to believe that Farmer Brown's boy had taken Shadow away and made an end of him. And because he wanted to believe that, it wasn't very hard to believe it. There was the empty cage. Of course Farmer Brown's boy wouldn't have gone to the trouble of trapping Shadow unless he intended to get rid of him for good.

"He's made an end of him, that's what he's done!" said Happy Jack to himself, because that is what he would have done if he had been in Farmer Brown's boy's place. So having made up his mind that this is what had been done with Shadow, he at once told all his friends that it was so, and was himself supremely happy. You see, he felt that he no longer had anything to worry about. Yes, Sir, Happy Jack was happy. He liked the house Farmer Brown's boy had made for him in the big maple tree close by his own house. He was sure of plenty to eat, because Farmer Brown's boy always looked out for that, and as a result Happy Jack was growing fat. None of his enemies of the Green Forest dared come so near to Farmer Brown's house, and the only one he had to watch out for at all was Black Pussy. By this time he wasn't afraid of her; not a bit. In fact, he rather enjoyed teasing her and getting her to chase him. When she was dozing on the doorstep he liked to steal very close, wake her with a sharp bark, and then race for the nearest tree, and there scold her to his heart's content. He had made friends with Mrs. Brown and with Farmer Brown, and he even felt almost friends with Bowser the Hound. Sometimes he would climb up on the roof of Bowser's little house and drop nutshells on Bowser's head when he was asleep. The funny thing was Bowser never seemed to mind. He would lazily open his eyes and wink one of them at Happy Jack and thump with his tail. He seemed to feel that now Happy Jack was one of the family, just as he was.

So Happy Jack was just as happy as a fat Gray Squirrel with nothing to worry him could be. He was so happy that Sammy Jay actually became jealous. You know Sammy is a born trouble maker. He visited Happy Jack every morning, and while he helped himself to the good things that he always found spread for him, for Farmer Brown's boy always had something for the little feathered folk to eat, he would hint darkly that such goodness and kindness was not to be trusted, and that something was sure to happen. That is just the way with some folks; they always are suspicious.

But nothing that Sammy Jay could say troubled Happy Jack; and Sammy would fly away quite put out because he couldn't spoil Happy Jack's happiness the least little bit.

XXXIII
Sammy Jay Upsets Happy Jack

A good deed well done often is overlooked, but you never are allowed to forget a mistake.

Happy Jack.

Sammy Jay chuckled as he flew across the snow-covered Green Meadows on his way to his home in the Green Forest. He chuckled and he chuckled. To have heard him you would have thought that either he had thought of something very pleasant, or something very pleasant had happened to him. Once he turned in the direction of Farmer Brown's house, but changed his mind as he saw the Black Shadows creeping out from the Purple Hills, and once more headed for the Green Forest.

"Too late to-day. Time I was home now. It'll keep until tomorrow," he muttered. Then he chuckled, and he was still chuckling when he reached the big hemlock tree, among the thick branches of which he spent each night.

"Don't know what started me off to the Old Pasture this afternoon, but I'm glad I went. My, my, my, but I'm glad I went," said he, as he fluffed out his feathers and prepared to tuck his head under his wing. "It pays to snoop around in this world and see what is going on. I learned a long time ago not to believe everything I hear, and that the surest way to make sure of things is to find out for myself. Nothing like using my own eyes and my own ears. Well, I must get to sleep." He began to chuckle again, and he was still chuckling as he fell asleep.

The next morning Sammy Jay was astir at the very first sign of light. He waited just long enough to see that every feather was in place, for Sammy is a bit vain, and very particular about his dress. Then he headed straight for Farmer Brown's house. Just as he expected he found Happy Jack Squirrel was awake, for Happy Jack is an early riser.

"Good morning," said Sammy Jay, and tried very hard to make his voice sound smooth and pleasant, a very hard thing for Sammy to do, for his voice, you know, is naturally harsh and unpleasant. "You seem to be looking as happy as ever."

"Of course I am," replied Happy Jack. "Why shouldn't I be? I haven't a thing to worry about. Of course I'm happy, and I hope you're just as happy as I am. I'm going to get my breakfast now, and then I'll be happier still."

"That's so. There's nothing like a good breakfast to make one happy," said Sammy Jay, helping himself to some suet tied to a branch of the maple tree. "By the way, I saw an old friend of yours yesterday. He inquired after you particularly. He didn't exactly send his love, but he said that he hoped you are as well and fat as ever, and that he will see you again some time. He said that he didn't know of any one he likes to look at better than you."

Happy Jack looked flattered. "That was very nice of him," said he. "Who was it?"

"Guess," replied Sammy.

Happy Jack scratched his head thoughtfully. There were not many friends in winter. Most of them were asleep or had gone to the far away southland.

"Peter Rabbit," he ventured.

Sammy shook his head.

"Jimmy Skunk!"

Again Sammy shook his head.

"Jumper the Hare!"

"Guess again," said Sammy, chuckling.

"Little Joe Otter!"

"Wrong," replied Sammy.

"I give up. Who was it? Do tell me," begged Happy Jack.

"It was Shadow the Weasel!" cried Sammy, triumphantly.

Happy Jack dropped the nut he was just going to eat, and in place of happiness something very like fear grew and grew in his eyes. "I—I don't believe you," he stammered. "Farmer Brown's boy took him away and put an end to him. I saw him take him."

"But you didn't see him put an end to Shadow,"

declared Sammy, "because he didn't. He took him 'way up in the Old Pasture and let him go, and I saw him up there yesterday. That's what comes of guessing at things. Shadow is no more dead than you are. Well, I must be going along. I hope you'll enjoy your breakfast."

With this, off flew Sammy Jay, chuckling as if he thought he had done a very smart thing in upsetting Happy Jack, which goes to show what queer ideas some people have.

As for Happy Jack, he worried for a while, but as Shadow didn't come, and there was nothing else to worry about, little by little Happy Jack's high spirits returned, until he was as happy as ever. And now, though he has had many adventures since then, I must leave him, for there is no more room in this book. Perhaps if you ask him, he will tell you of these other adventures himself. Meanwhile, bashful little Mrs. Peter Rabbit is anxious that you should know something about her. So I have promised to call the next book, "Mrs. Peter Rabbit."

CHILDREN'S THRIFT CLASSICS

AESOP'S FABLES, Aesop. (28020-9)

LITTLE WOMEN, Louisa May Alcott. (29634-2)

THE LITTLE MERMAID AND OTHER FAIRY TALES, Hans Christian Andersen. (27816-6)

THE THREE BILLY GOATS GRUFF & OTHER READ ALOUD STORIES, Carolyn Sherwin Bailey (ed.). (28021-7)

THE STORY OF PETER PAN, James M. Barrie and Daniel O'Connor. (27294-X)

FAVORITE GREEK MYTHS, Bob Blaisdell (ed.) (28859-5)

ROBIN HOOD, Bob Blaisdell. (ed.) (27573-6)

THE ADVENTURES OF BOBBY RACCOON, Thornton W. Burgess. (28617-7)

THE ADVENTURES OF BUSTER BEAR, Thornton W. Burgess. (27564-7)

THE ADVENTURES OF CHATTERER THE RED SQUIRREL, Thornton W. Burgess. (27399-7)

THE ADVENTURES OF DANNY MEADOW MOUSE, Thornton W. Burgess. (27565-5)

THE ADVENTURES OF GRANDFATHER FROG, Thornton W. Burgess. (27400-4)

THE ADVENTURES OF JERRY MUSKRAT, Thornton W. Burgess. (27817-4)

THE ADVENTURES OF JIMMY SKUNK, Thornton W. Burgess. (28023-3)

THE ADVENTURES OF JOHNNY CHUCK, Thornton W. Burgess. (28353-4)

THE ADVENTURES OF PETER COTTONTAIL, Thornton W. Burgess. (26929-9)

THE ADVENTURES OF POOR MRS. QUACK, Thornton W. Burgess. (27818-2)

THE ADVENTURES OF PRICKLY PORKY, Thornton W. Burgess. (29170-7)

THE ADVENTURES OF REDDY FOX, Thornton W. Burgess. (26930-2)

BLACKY THE CROW, Thornton W. Burgess. (40550-8)

OLD GRANNY FOX, Thornton W. Burgess. (41659-3)

OLD MOTHER WEST WIND, Thornton W. Burgess. (28849-8)

A LITTLE PRINCESS, Frances Hodgson Burnett. (abridged) (29171-5)

THE SECRET GARDEN, Frances Hodgson Burnett. (abridged) (28024-1)

THE GLASS MOUNTAIN AND OTHER POLISH FAIRY TALES, Elsie Byrde. (41306-3)

THE ADVENTURES OF PINOCCHIO, Carlo Collodi. (abridged) (28840-4)

THE STORY OF KING ARTHUR, Thomas Crawford (ed.). (28347-X)

ROBINSON CRUSOE, Daniel Defoe. (28816-1)

THE STORY OF POCAHONTAS, Brian Doherty. (28025-X)

THE THREE MUSKETEERS, Alexandre Dumas, père. (abridged) 28326-7

FAVORITE UNCLE WIGGILY ANIMAL BEDTIME STORIES, Howard R. Garis. (40101-4)

UNCLE WIGGILY BEDTIME STORIES, Howard R. Garis. (29372-6)

THE STORY OF THE NUTCRACKER, E. T. A. Hoffmann. (abridged) (29153-7)

THE LEGEND OF SLEEPY HOLLOW AND RIP VAN WINKLE, Washington Irving. (28828-5)

Favorite Celtic Fairy Tales, Joseph Jacobs. (28352-6)

Cinderella and Other Stories from "The Blue Fairy Book," Andrew Lang. (29389-0)

Nonsense Poems, Edward Lear. (28031-4)

Anne of Green Gables, L. M. Montgomery. (abridged) (28366-6)

A Dog of Flanders, Ouida (Marie Leprince de Beaumont). (27087-4)

Peter Rabbit and 11 Other Favorite Tales, Beatrix Potter. (27845-X)

Favorite Russian Fairy Tales, Arthur Ransome. (28632-0)

Black Beauty, Anna Sewell. (abridged) (27570-1)

Aladdin and Other Favorite Arabian Nights Stories, Philip Smith (ed.) (27571-X)

Favorite North American Indian Legends, Philip Smith (ed.). (27822-0)

Favorite Poems of Childhood, Philip Smith (ed.). (27089-0)

Irish Fairy Tales, Philip Smith (ed.). (27572-8)

A Child's Garden of Verses, Robert Louis Stevenson. (27301-6)

Kidnapped, Robert Louis Stevenson. (abridged) (29354-8)

The Bear That Wasn't, Frank Tashlin. (28787-4)

Huckleberry Finn, Mark Twain. (abridged) (40349-1)

The Prince and the Pauper, Mark Twain. (abridged) (29383-1)

Tom Sawyer, Mark Twain. (abridged) (29156-1)

Favorite Christmas Stories, Poems and Carols, Candace Ward (ed.) (28656-8)

The War of the Worlds, H. G. Wells. (abridged) (40552-4)

Paperbound unless otherwise indicated. Available at your book dealer, online at **www.doverpublications.com**, or by writing to Dept. 23, Dover Publications, Inc., 31 East 2nd Street, Mineola, NY 11501. For current price information or for free catalogs (please indicate field of interest), write to Dover Publications or log on to **www.doverpublications.com** and see every Dover book in print. Each year Dover publishes over 500 books on fine art, music, crafts and needlework, antiques, languages, literature, children's books, chess, cookery, nature, anthropology, science, mathematics, and other areas.

Manufactured in the U.S.A.